HONEY IN THE CARCASE

ALSO BY JOSIP NOVAKOVICH

HONEY IN THE CARCASE

JOSIP NOVAKOVICH

DZANC
BOOKS

5220 Dexter Ann Arbor Rd.
Ann Arbor, MI 48103
www.dzancbooks.org

First US edition: February 2019

Library of Congress Cataloging-in-Publication Data

Names: Novakovich, Josip, 1956- author.
Title: Honey in the carcase : stories / by Josip Novakovich.
Description: Ann Arbor, MI : Dzanc Books, [2019] | Short stories.
Identifiers: LCCN 2018040060 | ISBN 9781945814471
Classification: LCC PS3564.O914 A6 2019 | DDC 813/.54--dc23
LC record available at https://lccn.loc.gov/2018040060

Printed in the United States of America

10 9 8 7 6 5 4 3 2 1

For Joseph and Eva

TABLE OF CONTENTS

HONEY IN THE CARCASE

IVAN MEDVEDICH was washing his silvery mustache after eating a slice of dark bread with honey when a whistle cut through the air, deepened in frequency, and sank into an explosion that shook the house so that a bar of soap slid from the mirror ledge into the sink.

"Lord have mercy!" his wife Estera said. "What was that?"

"The Chetniks, what else."

Soon, another whistle and another explosion.

"Run for cover!" Estera shouted.

"What cover? This is the safest place in the house."

Ivan had built the house alone—actually, with a little help from his oldest, flat-footed son, Daniel, who had groaned more than he worked. It took Ivan twenty years of careful labor to finish the house, but one thing he had skipped: a cellar, perhaps because snakes had nested and floods crept into the cellar of his childhood home. *God is my fortress and my strength* was his motto. But now, in addition to God, a cellar would help.

He turned off the lights and prayed, and after his last Amen, no bombs fell for the rest of the night.

Next morning, Estera walked to the bakery early, because after six o'clock, the dark whole wheat disappeared and only milky white, soft, cake-like bread, as expensive as sin, remained.

The old baker's wife said nothing, handing her a two-kilo loaf as usual. When Estera exited, she heard a dog howl and then a high-pitched whistle. A bomb fell in a ditch ten yards away from her, exploding with a terrible blast. Shrapnel flew over her head, shattered the bakery attic windows, and riddled the faces of the nearby houses, which now looked like lepers' foreheads. She walked home quickly.

If the bomb had fallen outside the ditch, the shrapnel would have flown low and struck her. She and Ivan concluded that God had saved her. Still, as Estera peeled onions that day, her neck twitched, jerking her head to one side. Estera had borne Ivan five sons. The youngest, whom she'd had at the age of forty-six, died because the wall between the chambers of his heart had collapsed. Since his death, silver streaked her hair.

Ivan played the violin by heart. Estera chopped onions. Tears from the onion fumes glazed their eyes. Tears slid down their cheeks like little eyes, mirroring knives and violins. Ivan walked out to the rabbit cages. The rabbits' split lips quickly drew grass into their mouths. He took a white rabbit by its long ears and held it in the air. He had often petted the rabbit, so the rabbit was not scared, not even as his fist drove into its neck. The rabbit twitched several times and went limp. He shuddered and walked into the house and laid the rabbit on the table to cool. "You skin it this time," he said.

That day he could not eat rabbit, his favorite meat, for the first time in his life; he ate only bread with honey, old honey that had crystallized into white grains.

At dusk, more whistles, and a dozen blasts, all in the near neighborhood. It went on like that for a week—blasts at dusk and at twilight. In their street, a large crater loomed between two shattered houses.

When Ivan cautioned Estera not to go early in the morning to buy bread, she said, "I am used to explosions."

He said nothing to that, but hummed a tune, sounding like the buzz of bees, and bees it was that he was thinking about. In his old pickup, he drove out to collect honey from his apiary, ten miles east in a meadow of wildflowers near an acacia grove. He put on a beekeeper's hat and gloves and opened the hives. His bees were so ardent that they had made honeycombs even outside of the frames; Ivan carved these additions out and stored them without draining the honey. He placed framed honeycombs in a circular barrel, a separator. Turning the wheel, he listened to honey slide out of the hexagonal wax trenches and hit the metal wall. He did not mind bee stings—he'd gotten more than a dozen that day—because he believed they benefited his heart.

He harvested alone. His sons used to help him, dancing around the honey separator like Joseph's brothers around the grains of Egypt. But now one of his sons was in Australia. Another, Daniel, his firstborn, worked as a doctor. The third one, Jakov, worked as a carpenter in Germany. The youngest, Branko, stayed at home, studying for his entrance exams at the school of agricultural engineering.

When Ivan returned home with three barrels of honey and saw his son Daniel, he rolled up his sleeve because Daniel always took his blood pressure, especially since Ivan's heart attack. (Ivan still suffered from angina pectoris but could not get a retirement settlement because his Communist boss hated him and, he suspected, wanted him to die at the factory.)

Daniel had not come to take his blood pressure. Instead, he talked about how, in the village where he doctored, Chetniks went door to door, beating up old Croatian men as though these men had been ustashas. "The Chetniks with skulls and crossed bones painted on their caps drove people out of their homes, stole TV sets, burned haystacks. They cut off three old men's testicles and forced them to eat them. One bled to death, the others I stitched up as best I could."

"You should leave the village," said Ivan. "Think of your young wife and child."

"A colleague of mine has invited me to work in the Osijek hospital."

"Are they going to have enough work for you there?"

"More than enough! Thousands of wounded." He waved his hand as though to chase away a slow, fat fly.

Before his parents and brother could react, he was out the door, in his wobbly Citroen. Ivan rolled down his sleeve and turned on the radio.

The announcer said Vinkovci was eerily quiet. *Eerily quiet* was a cliché in a newscaster's voice, but not so through the window when Estera opened it.

No machine gun fire, no car noises, not even birds singing; only a woman's wailing far away.

"Estie," Ivan said, "we must take care of the honey. You know how the Montenegrin poet says, *A glass of honey asks for a glass of spleen, together they are easiest to drink.*"

"What kind of poetry is it if it doesn't even rhyme? Give me no Montenegrin junk when Montenegrin Chetniks are bombing us."

Ivan let the honey sit in the barrels for several days, and then he scooped the creamy top—foamy, white, and exceedingly sweet. He was certain that this was ambrosia, the drink of the gods. He and Estera poured honey all evening long into glass bottles. Ivan looked back at the filled larder shelves and said, "It's good, isn't it?"

Just then a bomb fell at the edge of their garden so that the floorboards shook and the tiles on the roof quivered and slid, like teeth grinding. But the honey stayed calm in the bottles. Another bomb fell to the same spot. Ivan and Estera stayed in the larder, the safest room in the house because it had no windows.

Next day a couple of Federal MiG jets flew low, sharding people's windows, but no window burst in Medvedich's house. At night the light from houses on fire flickered through the shades that could not quite be shut. The red light on the wall seemed to be painting a message. The following morning, Estera wrapped a scarf under her chin and walked out.

"Where are you going, old woman?" Ivan asked.

"To buy bread."

"You shouldn't."

She walked out, proud of her courage.

Half an hour later, when she had not returned, he stood on the threshold and chewed a honeycomb with fresh honey. Chewing the wax calmed him better than chewing tobacco. The phone rang; it was the baker. On the bakery steps, mortar shrapnel had struck and wounded Estera.

Ivan hurried to the bakery. He lifted Estera—unconscious, her abdomen torn—and drove to the hospital. A doctor took a quick X-ray. Shrapnel had penetrated her liver. He dug in with his scalpel and gloved fingers, saying, "Too bad we're out of anesthetics." As he fished for the metal, Estera came to and swooned again. Just as the doctor tossed the bit of iron in the garbage bin, mortar hit the hospital, setting the roof on fire. Electricity went out. The doctor sewed up the wound while Ivan held a flashlight. They carried Estera to the basement, where the stench of crap and vomit hung about mustily.

For several days, Estera lay half-dead, half-alive, green in the face, unable to sleep, too weak to be awake. Ivan spent many hours with her but more at home, fearing brigands would break in and burn the house. He prayed but lost the meanings of his words in reveries and forgot to say his Amens. *Words without thoughts to Heaven do not go.* He missed his bees, abandoned behind enemy lines. As he drank his ambrosia, he decided that the next morning he'd drive into the eastern fields no matter what, even through the hail of bullets. But next dawn a bomb fell in front of his house, shattering the windows and digging holes in the stuccoed bricks. The gate collapsed. Another bomb fell in the backyard and demolished his pickup. The shrapnel pierced the house windows. Luckily, his youngest son, trembling on the floor, was unharmed.

A pharaoh did not weep when Persians slew his sons and raped his daughters because his sorrow was too deep for tears, but he did weep when, after it all, his ex-minister came to him in rags and begged for silver. Just so, Ivan had not wept when his wife bled in dirty hospitals, when his house had been nearly demolished, and when the truck he had saved for fifteen years to buy burst into pieces and shriveled in fire. But that he could not go out into the fields and take care of his bees, that made the cup—not of honey—overflow.

He wept in his armchair, in his wooden shoes, will-less, nearly motionless. As a child, he had seen on the outskirts of his village Croatian peasants, dead, their eyes plucked out. His father had forbidden him to talk about it since this part of history was politically incorrect—*am strengstens verboten*—to recount.

One afternoon four Croatian soldiers walked into Ivan's house and asked for Branko. He was in the bathroom, but Ivan said he'd gone to the university library. He was surprised to hear himself lie, but then he remembered that Abraham lied that his sister was his wife to save her from a marriage in a foreign land. That Branko should be a soldier struck him as absurd. Ivan had raised him on turn the other cheek. For years the larger boys beat him, broke his nose, yet he would not fight back. Ivan had complained to the school president, who asked, "Is your son gay?" That was all he offered in the way of help, so Ivan had to protect Branko, giving him a beekeeper's mask to save his face, and walking him home while boys threw stones and shouted, "Baptists, Claptists." Branko, who had grown up as a theological experiment, without any malice in his head, spent his days developing landscape photographs in the shed, his darkroom, and his eyes stayed watery and bloodshot.

Estera began to improve. Daniel took her to Osijek, together with Branko, but Ivan would not leave his house, as though it was his skin. On his block, there were fewer than a dozen people left, and in the city, out of forty thousand, perhaps three thousand had remained. Neither phone nor electricity worked anymore. He lived on water from a hand pump and on honey.

He had been a corpulent, double-chinned man, but in a month in which it was all the same to him whether he was alive or dead, he became a thin man with sharp pentagonal jaws, overgrown in a Mosaic beard. Perhaps he would not have eaten honey if it had not reminded him of his bees; he ate it in their remembrance, a sacrament to the little striped and winged tigresses.

One crisp morning, Ivan felt tremendously alert. He wondered whether he was about to die, since before death one could get a moment of lucidity, to summon one's family and deliver blessings—that lucidity was a sine qua non in a Biblical death, and he, a father of several sons, would of course have a Biblical death. Or had his diet cleared his coronary arteries? The following day, since he still felt lucid, he concluded that honey had healed his heart.

He biked to see his brother David, the carpenter, in Andriasevci, in their father's house, ten miles away. On the way, he saw starved shaggy cattle roaming, masterless. Horses rotted in dried-up sunflower fields. Blind dogs stumbled into trees. Cats with red eyes purred so loudly that he could hear them even as he rode over cracking branches. Heads of wheat bent in the fields like contrite sinners; nobody harvested them.

David and Ivan hugged and kissed as brothers. After they had slurped rosehip tea, David said, "I have presents for you: one coffin for Estera and one for you. Come, take a look!"

"What? But Estera is alive. And I am all right."

"Of course. But in case you get killed, you won't be dumped in a mass grave if you have a coffin with your name."

The next morning, Ivan decided to go back to Vinkovci. As if he had not thought about death enough, or seen it enough, that his young brother—who used to spend most of his time making tambourines and singing—should see the world as a plantation of coffins, incensed him against the invading armies. He rode through the groaning countryside.

From the edge of the village, a black German shepherd followed him all the way home. There he wagged his tail, licked Ivan's shoe, and did all he could to endear himself to Ivan. Ivan gave him an old slice of bread and honey. The dog loved that.

Ivan stood on his threshold and stared at the horizon, dark blue with clouds. The stink of putrid animals, borne on an unusually warm wind, assaulted his nostrils. Smoke and gangrene.

And when the rains began, a ghost crept along the surface of the earth, not as an image, white and gray, but as a stench of wet smoke and pus. The muddy soul of the Panonian valley sought fire to solidify into bricks of a tower of Babel in which all languages would merge into one: Serbian. *Govori Srpski da te ceo svet razume.* Speak Serbian so the whole world could understand you, the Serb folk saying went.

He rode his bike to a foundry converted into a bomb factory and volunteered to make bombs for the under-armed Croatian soldiers. At the end of his shift, he always found the German shepherd waiting for him. One dawn MiG jets bombed the factory, mostly missing and hitting people's houses nearby, but they did damage it enough to shut it.

Ivan could finally take it no more, so he dragged a cart east, through Mirkovci. Now and then he stopped and scratched his dog's fur. He ran into a checkpoint made of stacked beer cases in the middle of the road. A Chetnik asked him, "Where the hell are you going?"

"I need to take back my bees from the fields."

"Bees?" The Chetnik pulled out a knife. "Your ID?"

"I have none."

"I'm gonna tattoo you so we can recognize you next time."

He pushed his knife against Ivan's face. The dog growled, ready to pounce. A Chetnik grabbed his comrade's arm. "Don't you see he's crazy? Let him get his bees." And turning to Ivan, he winked, and said, "God protects the crazy ones. I like that, bees. Bees!" When Ivan was a fair distance away, they shot at the German shepherd but missed.

That he had managed to pass surprised him. Perhaps the brigands had understood his beard as an emblem of Serbdom.

Ivan waxed the entrances to ten beehives and stacked them on his cart. When he passed by the Chetniks, they again shot at his dog, and this time they killed him. Ivan turned soil on the side of the road with a shovel and buried his friend. It took him five trips—and a dozen kilos of honey as the "road tax"—to bring home all his beehives.

Ivan built a brick wall around the hives. He melted sugar for his friends so they would survive the winter. Since he had seen Polish geese migrating south, a sign that the winter would be a long one, he thoroughly filled the cracks in the hives with frame wax.

For hours he listened to the congregation of bees. They were his revelation.

For the invisible things of him from the creation of the world are clearly seen, being understood by the things that are made, even his eternal power and Godhead... Yes, the invisible Godhead and his plan were revealed in bees. Bees fulfilled the Old Testament through the perfection of their laws and the New Testament through the perfection of their love for the queen bee, for whom every bee was willing to die. Ivan thought that even if he had never read the Bible, from studying his bees, he'd understand that a rational God existed.

He brought the bees several pounds of honey, apologizing for having taken it in the summer. He admired the heaven on earth, the earth in heaven.

His son Daniel visited and told him that Estera, although anemic, had nearly fully recovered. When asked to join her in Osijek, Ivan said, "Somebody has to stay here and protect the church and the bees."

The shack where his son had developed photographs had served as a chapel ever since Ivan excommunicated himself from the Baptist church. Likeminded Baptists and Pentecostals, for whom their churches had not been pious enough, used to worship in the shack with Ivan and his family, until they discovered that they were not like-minded. Nobody came now, but still, it used to be—and would continue to be—God's space.

Ivan played the violin in his chapel and studied scripture. He was disappointed that scripture mentioned bees only a few times and lions many times. It consoled him that in one verse bees got the better of the lion: *There was a swarm of bees and honey in the carcase of the lion.*

Another passage intrigued Ivan. *And it shall come to pass in that day, that the Lord shall hiss for the fly that is in the uttermost part of the river of Egypt, and for the bee that is on the land of Assyria.*

He whistled and hissed to call out his bees, but none came out. Then he made a flute from a wet willow branch, with a low note, and found a hiss that indeed excited the bees so that they came out and crisscrossed the sky into a mighty net. When they came back, they tossed out their drones, and they kept tossing them for days. A peculiar fratricide—that aspect of bee theologically troubled Ivan. Some element of God's wrath built in the natural order of things? In front of the beehives, fat drones with stunted wings curled atop each other and shrank; the ditch filled up with drones. On a sunny day, so many crows flew over Ivan's head, to feast on the drones, that the sky grew dark.

After a prolonged bombardment, a band of Chetniks came to Ivan's street. He was the only person living on his block. When he saw them coming, he unplugged the beehive entrances and hissed on his flute. At the same time, a bomb flew, with a low whistle, and fell in the street. It did not go off. Bees grew agitated and flew out into the street, where the sweaty Chetniks, having loaded his neighbor's furniture on a truck, turned their eyes to Ivan's house.

Thousands of bees covered each brigand, giving him the appearance of an armored medieval knight. The brigands ran helter-skelter, dropping their weapons. One staggered in circles and fell dead in front of Ivan's house. He kept swelling even after the rigor mortis gripped him.

TUMBLEWEED

Sleepy from spending a night at a truck stop near Rapid City—in dull debates with a couple of hairy potheads about whether there could be another Prohibition in the States and another Revolution in the Soviet Union—I stood on the shoulder of Interstate 90 with my thumb up. My arm began to hurt, and after an hour or so I sat on the side of the road, propping my arm on my backpack. Two hours later I lay on the shoulder and lifted my right leg, barefoot, sticking up my large toe.

I was standing up again when a pickup braked; its tires squealed and smoked, painting gray asphalt black. I climbed into the truck and faced a drooping blond moustache and weathered skin under a leather hat with a snake brim. A black gun on the seat made me hesitate; I didn't shut the door behind me.

"What you waiting for? You aren't Iranian, are you?"

"No." My feet crunched through a bunch of empty cans and fumbled over a hunting rifle.

"At first sight, I thought you were. I'm not gonna stop for some Iranian shithead. But then I thought, so what if he's an Iranian, I could blow his brains out—do a service to the world. But you aren't Iranian?"

"No, I'm glad to say."

"Have a beer, then. Where you going?"

"New York."

"That's a sick town. If I was you, I wouldn't go there. I could take you to Iowa, to I-80, how would that be?"

"Tremendous," I said.

"I'm driving to Missouri to visit my ol' man. It's lonely down there, so I'm taking him a toy." He pointed at a gray snowmobile in the back of the pickup.

"It's summer," I said.

"So what? Soon it'll be winter. For old folks, time passes fast. But for us fuckers on this freaking road, it's different. Man, I hope you're fun."

I glanced at the gun.

"Oh, this thing? Don't worry about it. It's for rattlesnakes. Hypnotizes them. Just keep it circling in front of their eyes, their heads follow. Once the sucker's got the rhythm, you pull the trigger. Head busts like a tomato. Thirsty?" He offered me another can.

I slid my thumbnail beneath the opener, and the smell of yeast popped out. For a while we didn't speak. On one side of the road, a field of wavy alfalfa seemed to spin clockwise; in another, a herd of Angus cows rotated counterclockwise. Not all the cows faced the wind.

Brown clouds of dust made the horizon hazy. Little dry, wiry bushes, like skeletons of globes, bounced over the road and collected on the fences alongside.

"What are these weeds?"

"Russian thistle. You've got an accent. Where did you say you were from? You aren't from Iran?"

"I didn't say I was from anywhere. Yugoslavia."

"How do you like it here? Much better than Czechoslovakia, isn't it?"

"I imagine it is."

"I've never been to Czechoslovakia…"

"Neither have I."

"Man, don't you joke like that with me, you just told me you're a Czecho."

"Yugoslav."

"Well, how'd you get out?"

"Simple," I said. "Cut the electrical wires with a pair of scissors, swam across a river into Austria, took hot gunfire the whole way." I considered pulling up the sleeve of my T-shirt to pass off my smallpox vaccination scars as bullet wounds, but I didn't have the energy to sustain such bullshit.

"At least in this country we have democracy," he said.

I leaned over the speedometer, staring at the hand that trembled around ninety.

"Don't worry," he said. "I don't believe in cops. Dig me a beer out of the cooler. Grab one for yourself."

We drank more than a case of beer, and then, for refreshments, stopped at a pitch-dark country bar and had a couple shots of Jack Daniel's. He kept laughing that he was on the road with a commie "from Yugoslavakia."

"It's pretty cold in Yugoslavakia, isn't it?"

"No, Yugoslavia's on the Mediterranean," I said. *Or used to be*, I might have added.

"Shit. The Russians have got so far." He took off his hat, wiped his white forehead with a red handkerchief. About half a dozen Minnesotans at the bar insisted I have a double shot of vodka, so I wouldn't feel too far from home.

Back in the pickup, the sunlight was unbearably bright. Hawks floated on the updrafts over grassy pastures nursing placid ponds. A hawk dove into the grass, and then slowly and heavily rose from it, its talons empty.

He swallowed a white pill and gave me one too. "Amphet-amines. A good invention, helps you drink more." A black cor-vette passed us. He sped up to 110, and, passing the Corvette, made the international "fuck you" sign to the driver. "Nobody passes me, I mean, nobody. Not even a cop gets away with that shit."

"Have you ever gotten a ticket?" I asked. Instead of answer-ing, he opened his right palm; I popped a can and placed it in his hand.

"So how come you don't got no wheels?" he asked me sym-pathetically, perhaps imaging that I was stripped of my license for heroic driving.

"Too much time at school," I said. "Hoped I'd save some money this summer, working the oil fields, except I couldn't find enough work. I'd heard you could make tons down here."

"You should've run into me before. I run rigs up in Montana. What work can you do?"

"Just a worm."

"That's okay. You could make a derrickman pretty fast if you aren't scared of heights. A little overtime, you'd be cracking fifty grand a year. I make about eighty grand, more than a fucking dentist in LA."

"It must be a great feeling. All the bucks."

"Better than getting laid."

"I couldn't compare. I haven't gotten laid since Ford was president, and I haven't ever made real money."

"Shit, as a drummer in Chicago, I got puss every night with a different woman—sometimes two, three at a time. We'd go into a hotel room, smoke weed, and bang! I screwed more in a year than a hundred average men in their lives. You'll never lay as many women as I did, I don't care how much education you got."

A green and white IOWA sign loomed huge above us. A small black-and-white sign stood on the side of the road: SPEED LIMIT 55. MOBILE HOMES 50.

"So you study in New York?"

"Yeah, Columbia."

"Don't crap me. That's a school for rich kids—all you got is your useless dick."

"I do study there. What can I say? The rich kids are the undergrads."

"So you think you're smart? Can't get laid, can't do better than work as a worm." He laughed. "A pinko at Columbia, you tell that to my gran'ma, not me!"

For a while, we didn't talk. Then he said, "Well, I'm gonna crash somewheres around here. I don't know about you, but I'm wasted. Why don't you get out here?" He braked suddenly, swerved on the shoulder and nearly into the cornfield.

"I thought you'd get me to I-80," I said.

"Out!"

I barely had enough time to get my backpack out of the bed. My notebook fell out and slid under the snowmobile. The pickup started quickly, the tires shooting gravel and soil in low trajectories twenty yards down the shoulder. The red sun was sinking into the cornfield. I realized my notebook was gone, and with it my novel of two hundred pages, a romance of sorts, which I was sure would be published by Second Chance at Love, Inc., and fetch me fifteen grand, maybe twenty.

Unsteady, I stuck my thumb up and looked around. A green LEMARS sign with a couple of rusty holes from bullets.

A truck siren hooted at me like a lonely freight train—as if I hadn't calculated there was enough time for me to cross the road to the gas station, where I asked about a bus that would get me to I-80. The attendant ignored me while pumping into a large Chevy filled with the wide, ruddy faces of an extended family. "Is there a bust...eh, bus stop around here?" No answer, so I shouted, "Are there any Christians around here?"

The husky gas attendant looked at me. "Christians? Listen, man. If you don't leave the premises pronto, I'm gonna call the cops. They'll tell you about Christians."

"But you must know Christ's teachings. He may even be your Lord, your personal Savior?"

"Get lost, ya hear!" shouted the man, while a Chevy load of sunflower faces watched us.

I staggered into the motel and asked about the bus terminal—three miles down the road, a little too far for me—and about a single room for the night—twenty ninety-five, a little too much.

Stepping out, I was blinded by bright lights. I missed the last step and sank, jolting the slipped disk in my back—potentially a capital injury, if I'd promptly sought workmen's comp from the construction company. There were two police cars waiting, three or four cops with beer paunches protruding authoritatively into the darkness outside the scope of the beams of light. Not happy with the limelight, I sidled sideways.

"Sir, stay where you are. There's been complaints about you."

"About me? How do you know it was about me?"

"Driver's license, please."

"But I'm not driving."

"I need it to identify you."

"I've got a green card."

"No driver's license." The cop's tone made it sound like grounds for execution. "We've got to test you. Drunk as a skunk, seems to me."

"I don't want to be tested. I am drunk, isn't that good enough? Isn't the freedom to get drunk at the root of democracy? Pursuit of personal happiness is guaranteed by the Constitution."

"Come now, it'll be better for you. Close your eyes. Bring the tip of your index finger to your nose."

"I don't want to. I *am* drunk, and so what? I'll bet you lift one or two yourself now and then, when you get home after a dull day of work, with your wife in pajamas."

"Bring that finger to your nose!" The cop was shouting now. The other one clanked a pair of handcuffs melodiously. So I followed orders, and it seemed to me I did a pretty good job, damn near hitting my nose, and only once my right eye. My eyeball hurt, but not badly.

"All right, now walk the straight line—put one foot right in front of the other." I did that too, and didn't fall. My assessment of the results must have differed from theirs: the melody-maker put the cuffs on my hands, and two cops shoved me into a car. They turned on the siren and drove me around the town several times to brag about having caught a menace to law and order. I felt honored. It was attention, certainly more of it than you get standing on the shoulder of the road, passed by all sorts of people.

They led me into a police station, doing a pretty good imitation of TV cops escorting a murderer. In a room, a thin investigator sitting behind the desk asked me to empty my pockets. He examined all the things on the table one by one, as if he hadn't seen the likes. He found my registered alien card especially fascinating, though I didn't think much of my photo; I had a large pimple on the tip of my nose from the unbearable heat in Miami, where I had immigrated.

He asked me what I was doing in Iowa, and I told him I was part of the labor force in retreat. We were defeated near Laramie,

Wyoming, because of the oil glut, no doubt an Iranian swindle. My anti-Iranian comment didn't seem to placate him. He asked, "Don't you know it's illegal to be intoxicated in public?" I said I didn't. "Don't you know it's illegal to hitchhike in Iowa?"

"But how else are you going to get around if you can't afford a car? That's discrimination against the poor."

"We're not the welfare department. For your own good, to protect you and others, we'll put you in jail for the night until you sober up."

He said this in a friendly voice, like a doctor sending a patient to a hot springs in the Alps to cure rheumatism. That made me feel pretty good, thinking I'd have a free night.

"And in the morning, you'll have to go to court and pay a fine."

"A fine? I have hardly any cash. I just have this check from working on coalmine silos in Wyoming…"

"Maybe you can get someone to wire you money," he said, turning my student ID over and cleaning his nails with it. Now I felt humiliated. So far it had all seemed sort of fun, so much bustle and bright activity, but now, on account of thirty bucks, tears welled up in my nose so that I sniffed and sniffed, clearly under severe emotional strain.

Another cop came by and said, "Give me your belt and shoelaces."

"Shoelaces?"

"So you don't kill yourself."

"I am not depressed," I said. "Besides, my shoelaces are rotten." To demonstrate, I tugged at one, which instantly snapped. "See, you couldn't even hang a cat with these." But there was no arguing; I had to surrender my shoelaces.

Holding my biceps, a cop led me into an empty cell. Neon light emanated from the ceiling. The faucet water was hot; it didn't alleviate my dehydration and headache. Although even the stool was hot, I sat on it and remained in that philosophical attitude for hours, as if posing for a post-modern replica of Rodin's gloomy sculpture. Then I lay on a hard wooden bench in the middle of the room—I guess it was supposed to be a spartan bed—and tried to sleep. I was nauseated. My bones, eyes, and unidentified organs hurt.

When it seemed it must be at least noontime of the following day, I began to bang against the metal door, staring through the barred window. Soon some other admirable citizens joined me, and we hollered, screamed, and kicked the doors of our respective cells. I hurt my toe kicking the door and wondered whether I could sue the U.S. government for compensation.

After a quarter-hour jam session, a guard appeared and asked us what we wanted. We all wanted to drink and to eat. The guard brought us some frosty donuts with orange juice. The donuts were sticky and the orange juice tasted of flour.

A guard led me into the courthouse, a large room with some kind of wood paneling. A well-fed woman showed up in a black gown, took a small polished wooden hammer, and banged with it on the table. She asked me to raise my hand and swear. I swore all the judge wanted, and even thought of contributions. I had to keep my right arm raised; my left was employed in keeping my trousers from sliding down. The cops had forgotten to give back my belt; judging by the appearance of most of the cops and the judge, belts were not a necessity in Iowa. The judge asked me whether I was guilty of public intoxication.

"I am not guilty. It's pretty natural to be drunk."

"Answer my questions straight, to avoid further inconvenience."

She repeated her question. She seemed persistent, so I agreed to plead guilty, to get out of the tiresome place. I had to pay thirty bucks to a cashier—a cheerful woman behind the glass partition who slid me half a dozen papers to sign, with the joy and generosity of a person distributing prizes after a golf tournament. I varied my signatures to break the monotony.

I got back my belt and my shoelaces. I tried to pass the tip of the shoelaces through the appropriate holes in my sneakers. My hand trembled from the hangover; I was like an old man who cannot pass a thread through the eye of a needle. A policeman observed my struggles, and I looked at him angrily to mind his own holes. With my saliva, I pointed the tops of my shoelaces between my forefinger and thumb—the faithful thumb that had gotten me so many places—and coaxed the laces through the holes.

It was cloudy, humid, and awfully bright outside, so that the streets glared as if coated with ice. I got to the Greyhound bus terminal, bought a gallon of spring water, and sat, gulping the water loudly while I waited for a bus to Sioux City. An old man sat next to me.

"How much rain did we get last night?" he asked.

"I have no idea."

"Not enough, not enough. I sure hope it rains some more."

Since I didn't look worried about the submoisture of Iowa soil—I had enough worries about my own submoisture—the old man scrutinized me, and, concluding I was an alien, asked, "How long are you staying here?"

"Half an hour longer, just passing through," I said.

"Oh, that's too bad. Our town is small, but we got some things worth seeing—the most beautiful courthouse in the whole state of Iowa. Its interior is paneled in polished oak. Just beautiful." His voice had become gruff with patriotism. "But of course, you wouldn't have seen that."

I stood up, shaking hands with the fellow drunk for about half a minute. With the sensation of welcome, I climbed onto a steely bus, where about a dozen babies screamed for milk (or, maybe, for beer and speed).

Through the tinted glass, before the I-80 exit, I beheld quite a sight. A mobile home lay over a crushed pickup. An intact gray snowmobile stood beside them, like a faithful dog waiting for its drunk master to get up from the ditch.

OBSESSION

WHEN ROSE HUGGED her husband one early evening, she smelled Obsession perfume in his beard. She slid out of his embrace.

"You look out of sorts," David said. "Would seeing *The Unbearable Lightness of Being* at the Pacific Arts Theater cheer you up?"

After the scene where a wife discovers her husband's infidelity by the perfidious perfume in his hair, David cleared his throat. Searching for his hand, hers bumped against his hardon—after a sultry scene—proving to Rose that he lusted for other women. Now it was certain: one plus one. From a seat next to hers, a young man's knee protruded, touching hers, first lightly and then firmly and warmly. She withdrew her knee but felt the neighbor's knee inching toward her as a threat, a threat the man seemed to hide from her, and she from the man and from her husband.

The following morning, however, she could not concentrate on her therapy clients. A young man, a philosophy student, told her he would kill himself because nothingness was the source of being. *The philosophical solution to the problem of existence was nonexistence—to the problem of life, death. And what is the psychological solution?* he asked. *Love,* she answered. *What a cliché!* he responded.

That evening her husband remarked that since she seemed melancholy again, they should go out. A friend of his from college, a Cuban exile and painter, had just called from Saratoga, and invited them for an evening.

Ricardo welcomed them at the door in a bright yellow shirt with red and purple canaries. He cooked brook trout, seasoned with garlic and butter. Rose relished the garlic while David tried to extract bits of it from the fish. "Aren't WASPs terrible—scared of garlic!" Rose exclaimed.

David had brought along French red wines that made your tongue and gums contract as if you were chewing coca leaves somewhere in the Andes. Once all three blushed from the wine—they had no fear of blushing from conversation, so they retold bawdy jokes. *What did the elephant say when he saw Adam? "I wonder how the poor thing feeds himself"*—was the mildest.

When night came, beyond glass sliding doors, orange light bulbs turned the patio into a stage, announcing a feast to a tribe of short-legged raccoons. Rose put half of her fish through the door, though she had just praised the fish's succulence. Ricardo moaned that his culinary masterpiece should go to the vile band of robbers. Raccoons gnarled at each other, like large and selfish felines.

Ricardo asked the Thompsons how they'd met. In college, David was attracted by Rose's ballet-trained grace. David borrowed from friends, relatives, and banks. He drove Rose in a Jaguar to string quartets at the symphony hall. In his room, he played CDs when hardly anybody had heard of them yet. Her parents were impressed by him until they realized that he neither had nor would have serious money. David soon made good money as a car dealer, and then better as a real estate broker. She liked him—his style, his ambition, his speedy driving, his humor. She thought she loved him.

Now David bragged to Ricardo about his moneymaking schemes and elegant vacations. "Rose, we must revisit Venice, the most wonderful city on earth."

"I love how artfully gaudy it is," Rose said. "Ricardo, have you been to Venice?"

"The whole city is a colossal antique," said David.

"Venice is the asshole of Italy, riding on rotting wood," Ricardo said. "Why does half of Italy look like a desert? Because Venetians cut down most of the trees."

"The city is unbelievable," David said. "I'm going to take tons of photographs there. Would you like to write a book on Venice with me?" David asked Rose and played with her hair, pulling it behind her ear.

"Why don't you go to Venice with us?" Rose suggested, looking only at Ricardo. "It's nice to be with friends. We are less than a nuclear family, we are only a certified couple."

Luxuriously tipsy, Ricardo leaned back in his chair and said, "David, you are incredibly lucky to be married to such a beautiful woman." He drew a smoke out of his aromatic pipe. "You wouldn't mind posing as a female magician?"

The following Wednesday, Rose's day off, before they would again meet up for dinner, David dropped Rose off so she could take a swim in Ricardo's pool while David went back to work for a couple of hours. Because of her injury—a car had smashed into her Toyota, breaking her arm—swimming was beneficial for her. Ricardo came out and swam too. She lay offering herself to the Sun, whose rays licked her so that her bronze body glistened, seal-tight; her skin's fuzz of miniature sensors, she felt, could receive a touch without her skin being touched. The sensors felt Ricardo's gaze. She stretched her arms self-consciously, arching her back a little above her hips; her muscles tightened so that the cast of light shifted, dancing on her skin. She opened her blue eyes suddenly, startling Ricardo.

Flirting is a wonderful thing, she thought. *It sharpens your senses.*

Ricardo invited her to watch a documentary about India: wives cremating themselves alive after their husbands died. Just as she walked out of the house, David, out of breath, ran into the garden, although it was before five.

"You rush as though you don't trust us. And yet several days ago you reeked of perfume!"

Ricardo walked out too, and David said to him, "Let's move the party to our place on Piedmont. Some friends of mine are back in town just for the evening."

In the duplex, David informed the party of ten what a bad year it had been for the French vineyards; fortunately, David had wines from the good old days. Rose sat next to Ricardo, while David sat at the opposite end of the table. When somebody mentioned massage, Ricardo said he could give the best backrubs.

"Really?" said Rose. "I wish David would give me a backrub, but he just doesn't care for it. Can you really give good backrubs?"

"The best in the county."

"I don't believe it! Prove it!"

She nudged him with her elbow and pulled her blond hair in front of her, baring her neck and upper back, her shoulder blades. The music of Muddy Waters was loud, and so was the party's laughter. Ricardo's thumbs worked close to her spine, his fingertips on her pulsating back. Ricardo squeezed her muscles, trying to follow their contours, roll them, press between them. His cool fingers made her shiver. "You are right, I've never had a better one!...agh...so good!"

·   The conversations ceased. From the corner of her eye, through her eyelashes, Rose saw that David was trying to look nonchalant, and that people looked at her, David, and Ricardo, as if to figure out who was married to whom.

Ricardo's fingers stiffened, and she felt a slight tremor. He stopped.

Flushed, she openly stared into Ricardo's eyes. She gulped wine.

Someone proposed an ice cream run. Rose stood up, wishing to go, and asked Ricardo, "Are you going?"

"No."

"Then I'm not going either."

"Actually, I think I'll go," Ricardo said.

"Then I'll go too."

In the car, Rose and Ricardo were pushed against each other in the dark. Ricardo sat stiffly. Hot tingles ran through her skin.

Back at the duplex with vanilla and pecan, Ricardo sat on the floor close to a fish aquarium, away from the husband and wife, gazing at the scarlet fish gliding slowly as if they were sad, and perhaps they were, in their jail of glass. People sat on the floor and talked about insiders trading secrets. Inevitably, David began to talk about buying real estate in southern France. He drank more wine than usual; Rose had never seen him so drunk. *Serves him right, screwing behind my back. At least I am honest about my flirting.*

David called Ricardo to the bedroom and showed him a collection of ten thousand French corks, with squeezed purple tips, beneath his bed in a pirate crate. "You dream better with this stuff beneath you." From among the corks, David drew an antique gun and pointed it at Ricardo. "It works," he said, clicked it, and put it back.

On the wall in the bedroom hung photographs of Rose. In one picture Eric Clapton embraced her, his hand resting on her breast. She leaned her head against his neck.

"The Cream guy? I thought he was a born-again Christian!"

"It's him!" said David. "It was taken a couple of years ago on a cruise."

In the doorway, Rose laughed. "He likes to show it to everybody, as if it were something to be proud of. That was before I met David."

"How was he?" Ricardo asked.

"What do you mean, how was he?" she said.

"Was he a good conversationalist?"

"He was very quiet."

David embraced Rose in the same way as the man in the picture. "Isn't she a precious darling?"

Rose walked out into the garden, where she overheard their conversation through the open window.

"You really are a good friend," David said. "It's always fun to see you."

"Now," Ricardo said, "you may have thought there was something between Rose and me. I would never do anything because she is your wife and we are friends. Actually, I am sure she would have controlled herself too if I had made a pass—I could have made a pass with her hanging around the pool so much."

Rose did not like how they congratulated each other on being good friends—over her. Swollen egos! Probably many a husband wants to see his wife draw men, particularly men who are close to him in opinion, confirming his good taste. Perhaps all David wanted to see between Ricardo and Rose was a genuine desire in Ricardo's eyes. But not in hers.

The next morning, David and Rose had hangovers. David canceled his appointments. Rose could delay going to the office; her first client would come at one.

Her hair in a towel, she tiptoed out of the bathroom to the living room. David was closing a women's fashion magazine—it had just arrived in the mail—and awkwardly walking away from it.

"I didn't know you read women's magazines!" she said.

"I don't, but it's tempting to see the new fashions."

She hugged him, burying her nose in his beard. Scents of *Obsession* frolicked.

"Hum." She took the magazine, and when she opened it a strong stream of *Obsession* hit her.

She examined the last month's fashion magazines, and on a black surface, she saw greasy fingerprints, circles. Later, before she went to work, she clasped and pulled her husband's hand toward her lips as though to kiss it. She examined his fingertips: the lines formed circles. She thought she had caught him cheating, and probably he had only read the slicks. But why would he? To gaze at beautiful models?

At work she got a call from the parents of the philosophy student. He had killed himself. He stole a BMW and drove east, pushing semis off the road. He drove straight at the semis until he collided with one. She brooded, feeling guilty, although she knew that a suicide usually made everybody who knew him feel guilty.

At home, she ignored David. Instead of trusting him more after solving the mystery of the Obsession, she mistrusted him more: he was a liar. He even lied about not reading women's magazines. He had pretended to be rich before marriage. He cheated on his taxes. And she trusted herself even less. Ever since she believed that he cheated, she felt erotically obsessed. Was revenge erotic? She daydreamed about gentle sex, extra-sensory sex, unlike the rushed athletic sex with David. Shouldn't she experience it? Before marriage, she had slept with only two boys.

She rented a mailbox in a downtown coffee shop and put an ad in *The Guardian*. *Sensuous fun-loving blonde looking for an imaginative brute for discreet meetings.*

One reply especially intrigued her, not by what it said, but by how—on a laser printer in Letter Gothic. Not many people used that font; her husband liked it in personal correspondence. Of course, the font did not prove that Alexis Schwartzberg was in fact David Thompson. But her husband's printer tended to blur the seventh line of the text, and in this letter, the seventh line was blurred. That was too much to be a coincidence. Should she confront him? How would he believe that she had never placed a personal? Maybe they could meet and pretend that they did not know each other. She remembered a story from *Laughable Loves* by Kundera. A husband and wife pretend that they don't know each other. The wife hitchhikes, the husband picks her up, and they have a wonderful time as strangers getting to know each other. But suspicion that they could easily do something like this with strangers and be unfaithful alienates them. They realize that they are strangers. With the ad, what story would he give her? He would lie. So why bother confronting him? Clearly, he'd like to have an affair.

For a while, she recorded his odometer readings every day and tallied his accounts of where he went with the factual distances—ever greater and greater.

After a couple of weeks, she gave up and proposed that they take a vacation. She refused to go to Venice. She needed something wilder, something less theatrical.

They went to Peru. From a hot springs pool Rose and David gazed at the snow-capped Huascarán as if the sight of ice would refresh them. Embracing, they floated.

Outside the pool, as David rubbed coconut oil into her back, Rose talked. "You know, that peak used to be taller. But twenty years ago, an earthquake cut a chunk of the glacial tip, and the melting ice and rocks killed ten thousand people in Yungay in the foothills. And ten years ago, an earthquake shook a glacier off its top—see, the ice cap is flat—and a torrent of ice, water, and rocks crushed the town of Yungay, killing some thirty thousand people. The peak is now about one hundred feet lower than twenty years ago; at 22,205 feet, it's still the second highest peak in South America, and for that matter, in the Southern Hemisphere."

"You read all this in a guidebook? How do you remember the exact elevation?"

"Once you hear it, you cannot forget it—twotwotwo-oh-five."

"Your neck muscles are pretty tight. Does the town still exist?"

"Yes, people rebuilt it."

"How many people live in it?"

"I don't know—about forty thousand."

"You mean, you don't know the exact number? Not 43,419 or something?"

"No, I am afraid not." Rose chuckled, intertwining her fingers with his behind her back.

He kissed her ear, pretending to insert his canines into her earring holes.

"What are you doing? It tickles, ah, hurts! Stop it!"

"Don't you want me to be your earring?"

"Maybe the rest of you, but not your teeth!"

"You know the best thing about our marriage is that we have so much fun—we've built it on fun!"

Now Rose traced acupunctural meridians on his back, pressing her sharp nails. She found a spot on his back that, when pressed, made his foot twitch. "And you say I need to relax?" She laughed, a clear laugh that made him laugh too.

Sitting on the steps in the water, groggy from the steam, David went on: "Too bad we have to wear bathing suits. The hell with them."

"But the natives are clothed," Rose said. "You mustn't be insensitive to their customs."

She recalled impressions from three days before—straw huts on the Titicaca Lake, a tourist boat, a young Italian woman sitting opposite from them, her serene emerald eyes beneath thin black eyebrows in a face of clear lines, and full, wavy, calligraphic lips—she didn't blink, staring at David. Her clear features cut an indelible etching in Rose's eyes, an etching uncalled for. Although she couldn't recreate the fresh hue of her eyes, she saw her face clearly. David had stared at the Italian.

"What are you thinking?" David asked.

"Nothing. I can't possibly think in this heat."

"How old were you when you had your ears pierced, anyway?"

"Six. I didn't want them pierced, but my mother couldn't pass up a deal. At a supermarket, although I fought tooth and claw, she had me tied into the chair, and my ears were pierced at a forty percent discount. She said I'd thank her later. And..."

A crew of loud British archaeologists arrived so that David couldn't possibly hear what Rose further said.

"They are enlightened Europeans," David said. "If they skinny dip, we can too."

"They won't. Do you want to bet?"

The crew got in almost in . full apparel—jean shorts and shirts. David was distracted by their darkened teeth.

Next, a crew of guttural Dutch tourists came to the pool, and before Rose and David could bet, a bunch of naked bodies flip-flopped above them, and glistening wet breasts, buttocks, and balls floated on the water as though filled with air. David followed suit.

Rose said, "You are a born conformist."

"And you are a prude. Relax! Look how beautiful it is here."

"If I am such a prude, why do you keep track of the exact miles it takes me to go shopping? Or to work? You think I haven't noticed?"

"Come on! I keep track of your miles? More like you keep track of mine. After all, you like numbers."

A couple next to them made love in the water, the bearded dude leaning backward and an enthusiastic lean young woman astride him, leaned forward. Rose looked the other way, and David touched her. "No, you won't get me to do that," she said. "It's probably illegal."

She closed her eyes. She was excited by the unrestrained couple, but to behave like them would be too much.

Later, the couple chatted with David and invited him and Rose to visit at their hotel room. "We got some coke, the best coke in the world. Come, try it with us."

"Thank you, how nice. Rose, what do you think, it sounds like fun!"

"It's totally pure. The best high ever," the beard said.

"I don't think so," Rose said to David, ignoring the stranger. "If you want to end up in jail, just go ahead. I am not going."

"Oh, come on, don't be a party pooper!"

"Suit yourself. I am not going. You can go if you like, but if you do, I am going right back to Lima and then home."

That night, they didn't make love, and Rose couldn't sleep. David said, "I am going out for a stroll."

"For the Dutch treat?"

"No, just to clear my head."

"It would take much more than a little stroll to accomplish that!"

The next morning, they zigzagged through a crowded market place in Huaraz before their bus trip to Yungay, the starting point of their hike around the mountain.

As David dispatched his last bite of a fried fish and threw its fragile skeleton away, Rose said, "Let's buy a chunk of cheese." Her voice often seemed to come from somewhere deep, not only from her lungs, but from her soul. But now her slow voice seemed to irk him, and he said:

"No, I've had enough omelets and cheese sandwiches to last me till Doomsday. Anyway, there is no time for that. The bus will be leaving any second."

"No, it won't, you don't know these people."

"I know enough."

"We need some solid food, otherwise we'll starve."

"I am sure we'll run into some village where we could buy quails, rabbits...let's go!"

She fondled a large yellow disk of cheese. "*Cuánto es?*" she asked a creased mestizo woman. The woman had a condor-esque nose and the disinterested eyes of an arbitrator in a black gown, awaiting the prosecution and defense to state their arguments; and, upon hearing the question, the arbitrator livened up, her small eyes becoming large. Now Rose began to bargain.

"Come on," David said. "We don't have time for that."

"Relax! Take it easy! Isn't that your motto?"

Rose handed some money from her smooth hands into the old woman's hands, which looked like cracked soil in drought, despite the indigo veins—streams and rivers—swerving through the dry skin. The woman put the money into her bosom behind her black robe, took out some change, slowly, and handed it into the pink hands. Rose put it into her leather purse, which hung from her neck, and packed the cheese into her backpack. David helped her pass her arm through the back strap. Rose then took a picture of the old cheesemaker.

As they waited for the bus for a good five minutes, Rose smiled, and wondered, did David join the Dutch for a snort? For a little threesome? She decided not to ask him. Maybe it didn't matter. And after all, she probably would have smelled something on him, some feminine smell. The hippies used all sorts of ointments and smoked hashish in addition to snorting. He had probably wanted to visit them but didn't dare. David paced up and down, and said, "Where is the damned bus?"

A truck came, and the waiting crowd soon filled up the bed. Rose and David joined them.

A day later, before sunset, they were reposing on the side of a pure glacier lake, locked between Huascarán's blue rocks and on the other side a steep rocky mountain. Rose stared at the turquoise of the water with a thirst for beauty. The tint was the same as the woman's eyes on the Titicaca. No matter how much she gazed at that shade between blue and green, she'd never possess it. Her muscles ached from hiking in the thin air, and her stomach growled. Rose took out the cheese and ate, smacking her lips.

"That smells good," David said.

She did not say anything.

He took out a dry piece of bread and chewed it with an onion. "Could I have a slice?"

"No."

"Why not?"

"You said you wouldn't want it. I thought you were a man of your word."

"Well, yes, then we were in a rush."

"You didn't need to rush."

"You have more than enough for the whole hike."

"I know, but we might run into some hungry children."

"I am hungry."

"So what?" she said. She had finished her meal while David still chewed the rocky bread crusts. She filled her cup from a mountain brook which loudly rolled stones. She put a pill into the cup.

"What are you scared of? There's no bacteria in the glaciers!" David said.

Rose stared at him. She put one of her contact lenses into her mouth, and then back into her eye. David chewed his hard bread, his left jaw popping; on the right, she knew, he was avoiding a new molar crown.

"Well, it wouldn't hurt you to give me a slice," David said.

"No is no. You didn't want it then, and you can't have it now."

David went down to the lake and bounced flat stones against the surface, came back and chewed a wild onion.

The rocks of Huascarán were radiant with the setting sun, and the glaciers glared like a magnified diamond crown. The lake lost its turquoise, turning a blueberry hue.

Rose began to unpack a red tent and looked at him askance for not helping her.

"Are you sure you want to sleep beneath that colossal piece of detachable ice, that iceberg in the sky?" David asked.

"Why not?"

"If the glacier comes tumbling down once every ten years, well…"

"Nonsense. Once every ten years is one in 3652.5; and one night here, eight hours, would decrease it to one in 10,957.5." Whenever she was angry, she could astonish herself by how sharp she could be.

"That's still pretty high for me…and it hasn't happened in ten years, so…and if it does happen every ten years, and it hasn't, isn't it more likely that well, hum…" He swallowed and ate his words.

"Have a slice of cheese," said Rose softly.

"No, I don't want any."

"You don't want any? How come? First you beg me for it, and now you don't want any. Take it!"

"No, I don't want it anymore. I've just had a juicy dinner."

She stood up to cut a slice. "Here, have some."

"Fuck your cheese!" David shouted, and his shout echoed from the mountains, "ease, cease, ease…"

She dropped the knife and whirling around her axis like an Olympic disk thrower, she unleashed the whole sunny cheese at David's balls.

David lifted his foot with the reflexes of a goalie defending his net. The cheese hit the sole of his sneaker, protecting the possible origin of a long genealogy of future generations.

Rose danced like a medicine man in a trance, holding a stone in her hand, ready to fling it at him. David jumped at her. He grabbed her and squeezed her. Her ears and her neck turned red, and she growled, kicking his shins with her heavy hiking boots. David flung her on the ground and sat on her to keep her body immobile.

Her booted feet, free, banged against his back. David lay on top of her, intertwining his legs with hers. He gripped her around her neck with his elbow. She sank her red nails into his hand and ripped. The well-rasped nails cut to his tendons. David clasped his left arm around her neck, pushing her head with his right arm into the hook. She felt she was about to swoon, and her kicks weakened. Then David let her go and stood up. Blood dripped from his hand. Rose had a hard time rising. David staggered away, and he dropped to his knees, tying the strings on his backpack into tight knots.

As she stood up, she could see nothing on the ground level, but there was light at the tip of the glacier on Huascarán, which was echoed, diminished on the blue rocks. Tears flowed down her cheeks. "I'll never forgive you," she said.

"You won't have to."

He walked away steadily in the direction of Yungay. As he grew smaller in the distance, the world astonished her with its glacial beauty.

WOOL

IN VINOGRAD VILLAGE one morning, a girl named Anna rushed out of her backyard when she heard a high-pitched murmur, her hazel eyes turning green as she looked through the slanting rays of the sun. A lake of sheep was flowing down the hill toward her in waves, each wave with many voices, all voices together becoming a huge sorrow. (After spending the winter in the Pannonian plains near the Hungarian border, the flocks were returning to the Bosnian mountains—this was in 1969, a long time before bridges over the River Sava between Croatia and Bosnia would sink.) Shepherds with long sticks, dressed in rags, walked along their flocks. Black dogs bullied the sheep. Rams with mud in their hair often bucked thick back-twisted horns. Ears hung on the sides of mothers' faces as if the mothers had grown tired of listening to bleating, though it was they who bleated the most. Little lambs struggled to keep up with them, bleating several octaves higher.

Anna's neighbors stood on the roadside, at the edge of grassy ditches, and chewed pipes with their yellow dentures. Her father Noah stood behind her, leaning on a hunting rifle, his small blue eyes vanishing into the redness of his chubby face. "If any of these damned sheep run off the road into my vineyard, I'll blast the hell out of them." He probably forgot that the rifle did not work—it was rusty and jammed with mud. His free hand lifted a bottle of crimson wine to his wet lips.

Anna asked a shepherd if she could hold a little lamb, as small as a cat—its legs were long so that it looked like a cat on stilts. It had black nostrils and black circles around its eyes.

"Could I have it?"

"Give me three hundred dinars, and it's yours," the shepherd said.

"Dad, could you…?"

"Hungry monster, aren't you?" Noah said.

"I'd like to have a pet."

"What good can a pet do?"

"The flock's not gonna wait," the shepherd cut in. "Take it or leave it!"

"Three bottles of wine?" Noah said.

"Four."

Anna ran into the house, brought five bottles from the moldy cellar, and was about to hand them all to the shepherd, but Noah snatched two and said to her, "Can't you count, ass?" and to the shepherd, "Take it or leave it."

The shepherd looked down the road at the flock, which had passed, brown dust rising above it, and said, "Blood is worth less to you than wine?"

"What can you do with blood?"

The shepherd wiped his dusty lip, and his Adam's apple rose and fell with a click. "Fuck your planets, my friend. You got me!" He snatched the three bottles, and Anna took the lamb from his forearm, where it had perched chewing imaginary future grass. The shepherd walked in quick strides after the bleating brown cloud.

"Kid, we got us a steal. Have a sip!" Noah offered wine to his child. Anna rushed inside the house to play with her little lamb.

For days Anna groomed the lamb, gave it milk, walked it in the vineyard down to the creek, and rolled with it in the cricketing grass. She buried her thin aquiline nose in the wool. Surrounding the lamb with her long coppery hair, she created the illusion that her face and the lamb's were in a luminous tent.

The lamb was clean and averse to mud and could have slept with Anna if it had not rolled little steamy bronze-black droppings all around the living room. Her mother, Estera, wanted the lamb to sleep outdoors on a chain, like a dog.

Anna set up the lamb in the empty pigsty, in a nest of hay and old sweaters. The lamb often broke into the garden and ate lettuce, cabbage, tulips, and white roses. Estera was dismayed. Anna dragged green branches of various trees to the lamb; cherry leaves were the lamb's favorite, so Anna climbed two large cherry trees in the garden and sawed off branches and tossed them to the lamb, who wagged its tail and hopped like an antelope.

Anna often crawled around the animal on all fours, as if she were a lamb too. She scratched her head against the lamb's, pushing a little. At first the lamb dodged her head and ran away into a bush of budding flowers, but soon it began to press its head against Anna's. For weeks they gently pushed each other around the yard, but the lamb was growing stronger and stronger, and for all Anna knew it could have been a ram. She decided, however, that it was a female, and named it Tanya.

As soon as Anna came back from school, Tanya would lower her head, dig her hind hooves in the sandy soil, and grind her teeth, as if she'd chew Anna. Anna laughed at the challenge and went down on all fours, imitating her teacher, who catapulted and flew to collide with Anna's forehead. The impact of the collision threw Anna off balance, so that she rolled on the ground. Anna had a splitting headache and tears went down her cheeks.

She invited neighborhood children to play the same game with Tanya. They were astounded at the violence of the sheep, and none of them wanted to have their head butted more than once.

Soon it was summer, and Anna thought the best part of her life was over. Every Saturday night, her father got drunk. The first Saturday night in June, he came home at midnight. He shouted at Estera, accusing her of sleeping with the chimney sweep, and hit her with his fist over her mouth so that she bled.

Anna's younger brother Mato—he was eight, she was almost eleven—and Anna stood in the corner of the room, their teeth chattering, while their father smashed a chair over an old cradle, where instead of a new child Estera kept jars of plum jam. The cradle cracked, the jars burst, and the dark sugary tissue of plums oozed onto the splintery floor. "Coward!" Estera said.

Noah charged after her and slipped on the jam, while Estera jumped out the window. He ran after her down the gravel road into the woods. In nightgowns Mato and Anna ran after them, screaming to their father, "Don't, don't!"

They caught up with him. His tobacco breath rasped, wheezed, and he doubled over and panted, "My liver, my liver!" Mato and Anna did not respond.

"Don't you worry about your dad?" he said.

"You bet!" Anna said.

"How dare you worry about me? I don't need your sympathy! Chimney-sweep bastards!"

He grabbed Mato and Anna by their hair and knocked their heads together and kicked them, and his knuckles struck Anna's cheek so that her face blazed with heat. Anna ran to the pigsty and moaned, while her knocked-out salty molar swam in blood around her tongue. She cuddled up with Tanya and fell asleep.

The next morning, when Anna woke, Tanya was sniffing her hair and wetting her eyebrows and eyelashes with her cool nostrils. That refreshed Anna. When she walked out, she saw her mother sweeping the entrance to their red brick house; the polished stone steps glistened. No evidence of the previous night remained, and Anna thought that perhaps she was crazy to think all that helter-skelter had gone on. But it was odd that her mother wore cherry lipstick; though her lips were full, her lower one looked too full now, so she must have hidden the bruise. Noah was repairing old wine barrels, taking off rusty rings and putting on new ones, then hammering them down. His hands were unsteady, and the short nails kept falling from between his fingers into the dust, where he could not find them. In his hangover imprecision he missed most of those that didn't fall and he hit his thumb; he groaned and jumped around the yard as though he'd hit his toe. He stood at the side of the spindle, sticking his hand into a pail of cool water.

Anna helped her father mix chemicals, for spraying the vineyard, in a cemented hole in the ground with walls as high as her waist. The chemicals turned pale green. Noah saddled the copper carry-on pump on her back. In wooden shoes, she walked down the slope between the rows of vines, sliding here and there over snails. She kept pushing its handle with one hand and with another waved a metal-capped hose with small holes, smaller than needle eyes, so that the spray came out as a haze that bit her eyes. This went on for two days. Sunday Anna hated it, but Monday she did not mind because she could skip school, and her father would write a note saying that she was sick, which, as it turned out, she was, with a cold—headaches and a nose drip—so she skipped Tuesday too, free to play with her friend the sheep.

When her father wasn't watching, Anna took Tanya to the vineyard and spread the leaves of the vines so she could chew young bundles of green grapes, which, out of their sheaths, looked like homeless peas. Tanya loved the baby grapes, chewing quickly, rubbing her ears against Anna's knee, looking at her sideways, flirtatiously, with big moist eyes. Anna petted her, and each swallow the sheep made was to Anna as though she herself had swallowed ripe apricots.

Who knows how long their idyll would have gone on if Noah hadn't sneaked up on them, grabbed Anna by the hair, and dragged her into the yard. Tanya fled into the pigsty, but Anna couldn't, though she kicked her father in his hairless white shin. He pulled his belt off his pants, tied her to the youngest cherry tree with a rope, and whipped her, mostly over the back. The metal buckle cut through her cotton shirt. It was as though fire licked her. For a while he did not seem to know how to stop, though he took several momentary breaks to pull up his unfastened pants.

Anna became feverish and her sores became infected. She lay on her stomach, and her mother rubbed plum brandy into her skin to disinfect her. Anna gasped with the pain and then fell asleep, brandy sinking into her blood from everywhere, so that she woke up drunk. Anna missed a whole week of school, and then got an F in math upon returning—she had forgotten the multiplication tables. While Estera cooked vegetable stew, Anna had to sit at the bread cabinet and recite the multiplication tables not only up to ten, but to twelve. Anna hesitated at eight times nine, and Mato, who'd been cutting his initials in the table leg with a Swiss knife, shouted, "Seventy-two." Anna could not think what eleven times eleven made, and while she was coming up with the answer with help from pencil and paper,

Mato shouted, "One hundred and twenty-one," and added that thirteen times thirteen made a hundred and sixty-nine.

The whole day afterward he put on airs for being the smart one, until Anna trapped him below the lowest wire of a row of vines. Sitting on top of him, she opened his mouth with her hands, put a stone between his upper and lower molars so his mouth would stay open, and spat into his mouth until her throat went dry, and then she held his white tongue down with a stick and lowered a brown spider on its silky string onto his swollen tonsils. That *would* teach him to shout his tables!

Noah stayed on the wagon for the rest of the summer. He and Anna often sang folk songs from Zagorye, to his tambourine accompaniment. Every day he and Anna went into the vineyard, pulled out old rotten posts, put in new ones, and nailed the wires to them. If a wire broke, they mended it, using a long eight-wire twist to connect it. Her father ordered Anna to tighten the fence between the garden and the vineyard so that the sheep wouldn't eat the grapes. But for that, Tanya attacked the garden all the more zealously.

Tanya had laid the backyard and garden to waste. Big and beautiful, she pranced around the yard like a racehorse, looking in challenge at the stray cats and dogs, who kept out of her way.

In early fall, the grape harvest took place. For a week Anna missed school to tear grape bundles off bumpy vines, toss them in a bucket, and carry them to the barrel at the top of the hill. Afterward, she, Mato, Noah, and Estera danced barefoot in the barrels, sinking through the grapes, while the grape juice flowed through holes into smaller barrels, where it would mature—or degenerate—into wine. Their feet stayed purple for days.

They boiled grape skins and distilled the steam into a pale brandy, almost as strong as pharmacy alcohol, certainly as poisonous.

After the harvest, Noah went into a tavern down the hill, and when it closed down, he brought home a dozen drunks, including the bartender. They slammed the doors and hollered and swore, so that they woke up the family. Through a slightly opened door, Estera and her children lined up their heads, one above another, and stared at the red-faced men. Several of them arm-wrestled; others sang into each other's ears with spent voices.

The morning afterward, Estera and Anna went to pray in the Catholic church in the next village—the peculiarity of Vinograd Village was that it had no church of its own. As if to compensate, the villagers had scattered a bunch of porcelain blue-and-maroon Mothers of God and thorny bloodied Jesuses, sometimes amidst a vineyard, so that the incomplete Holy Family looked like scarecrows, but far more durable than the raggedy ones in rotten colorless dark hats with Stalinesque mustaches made of horsehair.

During the sermon, Anna detested the smell of ordinary, non-vine-growing peasants: a mixture of garlic, hay, sweat, and manure. She stared around at their venous, swollen, blistery hands, which, as if ashamed of themselves, often clasped each other. The thumbs with the blue nails of a peasant across the row from her kept circling each other. She could not follow the priest's slow reading, though now and then she grew excited when the words *sheep* and *lamb* floated and echoed in the dank space above twisted candles.

My sheep wandered through all the mountains, and upon every high hill…my flock became a prey, and my flock became meat to every beast of the field, because there was no shepherd, neither did my shepherd search my flock but the shepherds fed themselves, and fed not my flock….I will require my flock at their hand, and cause them to cease from feeding the flock; neither shall the shepherds feed themselves anymore; for I will deliver my flock from their mouths, that they may not be meat for them.

Anna was disappointed since the words did not honestly mean what they said directly, but something beyond the sheep, about Israelites and Christians. She thought this was abusive to sheep, to use them as pictures for people's own purposes. But she liked the verses that the priest read afterward. *The Lord is my shepherd; I shall not want. He maketh me to lie down in green pastures: He leadeth me beside the still waters....Yea, though I walk through the valley of the shadow of death, I will fear no evil: for thou art with me; thy rod and thy staff they comfort me.*

Anna sneaked out of the church. She climbed the large unsteady stones of a ruined Turkish fort, stared at glowing amber forests, and listened to the shushing and murmuring of falling beech leaves, each leaf floating like a bloodshot eye without a head to illumine. The fleeting shadows of the falling eyes gave Anna shivers because she had the impression that flocks of mice were running at her and up her legs. The flat eyes drifted into a swerving green river, and the river turned red.

On the way home, she passed her father's favorite tavern, with the cries of drinkers rising above the clanking of silver and china. She smelled grilled meat, and inhaled deeply because the smell was pleasant. She read the sign: "Today's Special: Lamb."

At home she called for Tanya. No answer. She looked for Tanya everywhere. She walked back to the tavern and peeped in. The red-faced bartender, with his greasy brown beard, laughed.

"What do you want, girl? Would you like some diced lamb?"

"Where did you get it?" Anna asked, her throat parched.

"Where? Your dad sold it to me; I gave him a good price, a very good price! We neighbors have to support each other..."

"You are a shitty pig!" she shouted, and the tavern owner ran after her. She grabbed a sharp stone from a heap of gravel on the side of the dirt road and aimed at the bartender's forehead. The blue stone hit its target. His face was bathed in blood, and like the blinded Cyclops after Odysseus, the bartender bellowed threats.

At home, Anna called her father names that he clearly could not believe she knew, though she had learned them from him. He grabbed her and knocked her head against the blue-washed wall. Anna kicked him in the stomach. He tied her to the chair and said:

"How do you think I feed you, brat? That sheep costs me a barrel of wine, with all the grapes you ripped off for her. And how do you think we're gonna feed ourselves? Don't you know that our grape harvest was lousy? I won't be able to pay taxes, and the government will steal our vineyard, and we'll starve."

"You're a murderer! A beast, pig..."

Father poured himself wine in an aluminum cup and drank it, tears in his eyes. He got up and pulled out a sheep's leg from the bucket, still bloody, and said, "Dear daughter, I'm gonna cook it. This is a delicacy, grape-fed lamb!"

Anna tried to spit in his direction, but her burning mouth could produce no saliva, and when he offered her a slice of lamb, she closed her eyes and screamed.

Noah sat with her a whole day. He chewed lamb stew with onions, smacked his lips, drank wine. And he talked. "During the war, I had to boil my leather shoes and eat them. I chopped them up in a thousand pieces. In the famine after the war, we got only Red Cross rice, so I became as thin as a rake and got TB. And look at you, how lucky and thankless you are, brat!" He sighed and then sobbed. "So eat, my daughter, eat, while you can."

Anna listened but still would not eat the lamb, not even on the second day. Her father slept by her side, and prevented her mother and Mato from bringing her plums and walnuts. He let Anna drink, but only wine. On the third day, when Noah fell asleep and snored in deep unrhythmic bursts, Mato fed her bread and milk, but Anna was so dizzy she could not keep her head up. In the evening her father woke up and tickled her nose with salted slices of grilled lamb. "Don't you want it real bad? I bet you do. Have a bite!" And with his thick fingers he pried her mouth open and pushed in a slice of lamb. She slammed her jaw shut as hard as she could, biting his thumb and forefinger. She spat out the flesh and blood—more blood had come from her gums than from his fingers.

Noah was so taken by surprise that he did not react. Estera came in and shouted, "Enough is enough! Sure, we could not have let her carry on with her sheep anymore, but you better stop!"

"She bit my finger to the bone!" Noah howled. "Quick, alcohol!" He dipped his fingers in a cup of brandy, and Estera bandaged them.

"I'll teach you a lesson yet, crap shooter!" he said to Anna.

"If you haven't yet, I don't think you ever will," her mother said. "You've taught her nothing but to hate." Her mother walked out, turning her rosary beads and muttering.

That evening Anna grew so weak and drunk that she could not resist her father pushing lamb into her mouth. Almost asleep, she chewed the meat and gulped it with wine, and it was amazingly tasty; the amazement alerted her senses, and when she realized what was going on, she spat and vomited. She wept in misery, for she had eaten of her friend.

It was nighttime, and as usual in the fall, a power shortage resulted in a blackout. A lantern on a chair cast a light, so that

Anna saw a light from below pass through her father's upper lip and nostrils, both made orange by the light that stayed in them. The shadow of his nose cast a pointed triangle across his bare forehead. He said nothing. He stood up, untied her, and marched out of the room.

Anna did not go to bed because she was afraid that when he got back he would beat her. She trembled for three hours, and as the church rang a brassy midnight, she grew calm. She could hear her father singing on his way home, hoarsely, lyrics of some forbidden regional folk song. Anna grabbed the old rusty rifle from behind the pigsty, and when he opened the yard gate, she struck him on the back of his head with the heavy handle. He fell on the brick-laid path.

Anna feared what he might do if he got up, so she hit him again, as hard as she could. Anna kept hitting and hearing crackling of bones, but she did not dare to stop.

LIES

MY BROTHER, only eighteen months older than I but old enough to have a crucial advantage, told me had an army of miniature soldiers. A whole aviation squadron was at his disposal. His soldiers were hidden deep in the Doljani Hills, which could be seen from the roof of our house. His airplanes could fly vertically, change into helicopters, change size, become invisible, fly 10,000 miles per hour. The bombs his planes carried did not exceed the size of BB gun bullets, but they were nuclear. A single one could destroy the whole school and the church. Any time, he warned, he could put an end to our sufferings in school, his present one and mine to come. This piece of news was very encouraging to me.

The squadron that he had in the mountains was not his only one. He had another one, a much bigger one, in Zagreb. This army had even more miraculous properties, the details of which I forgot in my torpor of amazement. He could tell me anything at all without any suspicion on my part. He could have told me, and probably did, that he could torpedo Hell from his base in Zagreb, the biggest city in the world, at least the biggest real city. We had heard of New York, but New York was on the level of Heaven and Hell. I suspected that Heaven, Hell, and New York did not exist, for even my grandmother, who lived in the States, never mentioned New York. Unfortunately, I think my brother had not told me that he could torpedo Jesus and Heaven.

It was necessary to see Zagreb and his military base. He refused to show me the closer and smaller base first, because he said he wished me to behold his army in full splendor. We slapped our junkyard tires with sticks and set out westward to Zagreb. The trip would be only about 140 km. If we kept a steady pace, we would be there in no time at all, for our tires could be very quick on the open road.

We rushed without speaking. It was already late in the afternoon and we had to reach Zagreb before dark. We advanced a block from home. Suddenly a terrible wind, such as I had never felt before, began blazing across the street, raising a thick screen of dust. The wind stopped me on the spot, and although I tried to leap through it, I could not move. I opened my mouth very wide as I was out of breath, but could not get any new breath because I could not exhale. My lungs were full. Gasping for air and not getting it, helpless, I enjoyed a cool sensation in my trachea and lungs.

We turned homeward. The wind carried us over the street. As soon as we crossed the doorway of our yard, big beads of white hail from the black sky covered the whole ground. The beads rebounded as if made of rubber.

I felt safe in the shelter of the doorway.

COUNTER-LIES

I THOUGHT there was something amiss in my brother's stories. It was strange to see the general of the most formidable air force in the world beaten by our mother. Besides, he hated school so much that by now he should have destroyed it with his air force, and yet he kept going every day.

I prepared to avenge myself, but I could not think up incredible stories that would be believable. However, my lungs came to my aid. After having been ill the whole winter, I was to go to the Slovenian Alps to recover.

My father and I set out to Slovenia by train. It was still dark and cold in the morning. Then a big orange sun rose in the east. Mist covered small valleys and glens, and the grass dew twinkled sunshine at us. The train was slow as it climbed over the hills outside of our town. My father told me I could see big mountains compared to which our hills were like anthills.

In Zirovnica, a small village in the Alps, we went into a church. After the service, my father introduced me to the brethren as his sick son and people patted me on the head. I saw several variegated pieces of paper slide from my father's hands into the hands of a man. A couple of minutes later he departed, leaving me behind. The man was my host, the father of a big family in which there were no children.

Bodgan, a young man of my host family, took me into the mountains. We visited a flock of sheep. He tossed salt over the grass and the sheep ate the grass in sped-up motions. We continued to climb. The trails were very narrow and I feared I would fall down a precipice. I had no courage to go on. Bogdan laughed and carried me over the narrow stretch. When we got high up into an open space, we could see incredibly far: mountains of blue-grey rocks and snow atop; yellow, green, and brown fields; several rivers merging into one. Houses in villages looked like flocks of sheep grazing calmly in the valleys; smoke arose from several tall chimneys: the steel factory of Jesenice. A long train like an earthworm was sliding into a tunnel.

"Look! The train is making a hole in the mountain!"

"No! It's a tunnel, it goes all the way through the mountain into Austria. See, there are people on the train, and there is no telling where they are going."

In lust for sight, my mouth was open and my saliva trickled down my chin. I lost all my fear and inched too near the edge of round, smooth rock. I began to slide over it. Quickly I lost curiosity about the world. Fear flamed up into panic as I saw the huge emptiness below me and the miniature world below. Bogdan leapt forward and grabbed me by my long flying hair.

One day later, Bogdan and I went into the mountains again. From a high vantage point, Bogdan showed me rocks in the valleys.

"These are safes where people keep money. Each family has its own rock. It is difficult to know which ones are safes and which only rocks."

"Are the rocks hollow?"

"The safe-rocks are."

"Then let's roll rocks from up here, and all the hollow ones will crack into pieces! Then we can gather the money and go to Austria through the tunnel!" I suggested enthusiastically.

Bogdan laughed loudly. I feared that he had lied to me; I escaped one liar only to run into another. However, I still believed there was money in the rocks. With the money I could buy ice cream every day, a real bicycle, and a bazooka to shoot down a passenger airplane so it would fall into our garden and I could see the engines, and moreover, see what strangers look like. However, I could not roll any rocks down the slopes, and Bogdan kept laughing.

In the village, I saw horses and avoided them. An old man took me into the woods and wanted to put me on horseback. I screamed with terror. Puzzled, he let me go and we returned to the village.

Bogdan showed me skiing grounds and cable cars.

"They are run by electricity. Electricity is an invisible river under high pressure. The river flows through wires and pushes the cars."

"I don't believe you. You are a liar just like my brother."

Several days before my father was due to take me home from my convalescent vacation, I discovered the joys of playing with water pipes. In my town we had no tap water. I let the water flow under maximum pressure and spurted it over my palm, over horses and peasants who passed by. I could not direct all the water onto them, and a good proportion of it spurted over my face and chest. It was all right as long as I could get some of it onto the passersby. After a while I was soaked in cold water. I thought I should not let myself be seen by my hosts while wet because I would disappoint them.

I hid in the fields behind a stack of hay. It was a cold, windy day. My hosts continued shouting my name for hours all around the fields.

Upon my father's arrival, I tried to present an image of health, because I thought that it was in the interest of general happiness that I should be healthy. But by suppressing my cough while my father climbed up the steps and entered through the door, I simply collected the ammunition for a vehement cough to greet him.

In the train on the way back, I was thinking about clouds that I had seen only about fifty feet above my head near the Three Headed Mountain. I had asked Bogdan whether I could catch a piece of the cloud and he replied I could not because the cloud was only steam.

When I faced my brother Ivo upon returning, it was time for revenge. I began to tell him stories about the miraculous land. Of course, they were all true stories.

"I caught a piece of cloud," I announced.

"How did you do it?" he asked me skeptically.

"It was simple. I climbed toward the top of the Three Headed Mountain—just a hundred meters within reach of the top, near a glacier. We were passing through the clouds like angels. I took out a pocketknife and cut a piece of the cloud off. It did not bleed. You know, you can cut a cloud into many pieces and each of them will be a new cloud. It was a very funny cloudlet. It told me all sorts of stories about the mountains it had seen. It spoke Austrian."

"So how do you know it spoke about mountains? And how were the stories funny if you did not understand them?"

"Hhhhh…hhhh…Bogdan told me it saw the mountains. He could translate Austrian. He translated some stories for me."

"So you must know many things about Austria?"

"Not really. Bogdan translated into Slovenian, and I could not understand Slovenian very well. He laughed so I knew the stories were funny. Anyway, I put the cloud into a matchbox to bring it to you—you know, the way our father keeps queen bees in matchboxes when there are more than one in a beehive. Now and then I opened the matchbox to see our princess cloud and to listen to Austrian. It could not stop talking. I began to trust that we were good friends and opened the box a little too much so that the cloud could see our town with me from the hills, you know, from behind the V curve of the Doljani Hill. The cloud jumped up from the box and out through the window. It went higher and higher into the sky, made several circles above the train, and I couldn't see it anymore. I hope it did not get lost. The sky is big."

My brother stared at me.

"At least I saw it and you did not!" I exclaimed in triumph. My brother's mouth was now open.

"I wanted to bring it to you. You could have listened to Austrian, too. It would have taught us Austrian. What a pity! What a pity.

"That's not all! I wish you could have been there! Even in the summer, there is plenty of snow in the Alps. You could ski. They have electric skis. If only you saw how quick they are!"

Since I wished to avoid explaining how the electric skis worked, I went on:

"But that is still nothing. They have jet skis! You can go uphill with them more quickly than you can go downhill with your rotten planks of wood!

"I fell down a cliff two thousand meters high! I fell only fifteen feet before I caught a raspberry bush." As evidence I showed my palms with fresh scratches from Slovenian rocks and a scar from the kitchen knife of my hosts.

"It is true, what our minister says happens before death. You see all your life in a second. I saw all my life in that small second, all the sins I had committed. It was in color. Every sin, every stealing, slandering of parents, having idols, all the bad thoughts I had, and all false testimonies! Wonderful! If you want to see yours, jump off the roof!"

As my brother stared at me with his mouth agape, I was happy. Now I am not sure whether he stared at me so because he was surprised that his younger brother was able to lie so shamelessly, or because he truly believed me. Either way, he did not jump off the roof.

PEAK EXPERIENCES

AT A SOHO PUB, David hosted a reunion of his friends from college. At midnight he stood up, and after crashing a glass of wine on the floor, delivered a toast of sorts: "You are all cowards and I am ashamed to have friends like you!" He overturned the heavy oak table around which they were seated. Pitchers of beer, jugs of Diet Coke, and glasses of wine crashed to the floor. David stormed out of the pub, leaving behind his stunned wife and friends—musicologists, musicians, and assistant professors of mathematics. He muttered, "What a bunch of wimps, drinking Coke! Shitheads, they are scared to relax and celebrate!"

The following morning, with a pulsating headache, he called up his friends, one by one, and apologized. "I'm sorry; I'd looked forward to seeing you so much, and I was just disappointed that it was so quiet. I had vodka before getting there, and…"

But apologies were not necessary. Nobody took offense. It quickly became an anecdote to David's credit: though David had betrayed his college-days' ambitions of becoming a pianist and mathematician, he'd remained real.

And to be fully real, self-actualized—and not because he thought he was in trouble—he started seeing a therapist, a woman decorated with Ivy League degrees and the authorship of a how-to book on self-control. Dr. Fisher. Her first question to him was, "What is your earliest memory?"

"I tried to bury my face in my mother's breasts. She pushed me away. I guess I was about three years old. I know I was only two months old when I was weaned."

"Do you feel your dearest ones often reject you?"

"I don't think so."

"Or do you reject them?'

"No need for either. We live in different cities." He recounted a brief autobiography: a foreign-service brat, born in a taxicab in Italy, a child prodigy. Mother, an alcoholic journalist with imminent deadlines; father, demoted from a diplomatic post to a university professorship. His voice deepened as he recounted that his father had lung cancer.

"How about love?" she asked. "What was your first real love?"

"When I was seventeen, at a New Year's Eve party, somebody introduced me to a girl I'd had a crush on for years. We shook hands and she smiled. That's all I remember of it. Next afternoon, a couple of my friends congratulated me. 'What for?' I asked, and they laughed. 'Don't play dumb, you know damn well what for.' Apparently, after she and I shook hands, we kissed and half an hour later we made love. In my drunken blackout, I remembered nothing of it!"

"Incredible, isn't it?"

"I'd thought that sleeping with her would be the highest point of my life. I felt sorry that I had missed my most important experience. I thought of quitting drinking. But then, it's such a good feeling—"

"You can relax more constructively." She rolled her neck and lifted her shoulders in such a way that her breasts roundly faced him. The graceful cure of her neck continued to her chin. He had an urge to bite her neck.

"So now where do you stand with love?'

"Of course, I love my wife."

"The way you rush in with 'of course' makes it suspect. Or maybe you do and you don't know it. Or you nurture crushes you hope you'll realize one day in a showdown, another black-out, so that you'll be safe from love. Since you drink habitual-ly—we won't say that you are an alcoholic, but you may be—you've frozen your personality at the stage of development where you began to drink. In other words, if it was at seventeen that you began to drink, you are psychologically seventeen years old. So you are likely to flirt and constantly have crushes: something constructive at seventeen, but destructive at twenty-seven, espe-cially since you are married."

As David listened to her, with a tremulous cowlick rising from his shiny round forehead, his hazel eyes sunny-side up, full lips part-ed, teeth milky white, he looked much younger than seventeen.

Usually she didn't talk that much.

At home David fantasized about his therapist. His wife, Be-atrice, was of course enough for him. She was wonderfully virtu-ous. For example, after her mother's death, she took over caring for her mother's nine cats. Six healthy ones she managed to give away, but three unhealthy ones, which nobody wanted, she kept. She nurtured a white tomcat who had suffered a stroke; he had no sense of distance, so that though he saw his food, his tongue and teeth missed it. He had to be spoon-fed. You couldn't pet him without him going into the tic of trying to bite his right foot off. Another, an asthmatic Russian Blue, coughed and wheezed and had watery eyes. The third cat died of feline leukemia, but not before Beatrice had spent about two thousand dollars in vet bills. To David there was something spooky about her cats, but he didn't have the heart to press her to get rid of them.

Beatrice had earned a B.F.A in violin from the New England Conservatory. She had gone on to study at the Paris Conservatory, but she quit. The strenuous practices seemed to her mechanical, militaristic, and dehumanizing; she had sought love in music, and in cruel perfectionism she did not find it. So she began to yearn to organize a family, the arena of love.

After marrying David, she couldn't give birth to a child. She underwent many medical exams, but David refused to be subjected to the humiliation of having his sperm counted. He claimed, "The money count, nor the sperm count, is what matters if you want to have a kid. Wait till we save enough."

Beatrice gave music lessons part time and continued to play music for love. Though not ambitious, she auditioned for the Hartford Symphony; the conductor offered her a place as first violin. She did not want a full engagement, so she subbed for the orchestra instead—quite frequently. She minded that her husband was so busy at work that he had no time for family. And when he had time, he was drunk. Now and then she knocked with her knuckles against his rib cage and said, "Open up!"

One midnight David tried to call his therapist. After her husband hung up on him, David called again and asked for Dr. Fisher.

"I must see you right now," David said to her; she yawned. "Why?"

"My father killed himself."

Ten minutes later, they met in her office.

"You know, through the mail he ordered a book in French about how to kill yourself in the safest way: how not to run the risk of survival. When I visited him, we read the book, chapter by chapter, and laughed. I didn't think he'd do it. When his cancer got worse, I thought he would become religious or something. But he didn't. He liked living without hope, or at least he gave that impression. He said, to make sure that he would kill himself, he would inject poison into his veins, lie down on the tracks before an oncoming train, and shoot his brains out—triple assurance.

"Last night, on the phone, he said that he had gone to the hospital Laundromat and a patient flashed his wound at him. The patient had tried to shoot through his heart, missed, and had a huge scar that he liked to share with people."

"Only one in three hundred attempts of suicide by shooting through the heart is successful. Isn't it amazing that people don't know where their hearts are—and if they do, that they cannot reach them?" Dr. Fisher offered him the solace of statistics and wonder.

A day later, the conversation continued in a restaurant with candlelight—as if his father were laid on the table. In a muted voice, David spoke with the authority of death.

"I visited his home in Watertown. After his divorce, my father changed nothing in the house, so it was as I knew it in my childhood, like a museum. I could follow his steps from the entrance to the laundry room. In the living room, he folded his raincoat over a chair, leaned his walking stick against it, and put his black hat in the middle of the varnished round table. I...I...you...well, everything of his was there, his character, but he wasn't. His clothes were still wet in the washer. He never got to put them in the dryer. He fired through his brain. The bullet made a hole in the reproduction of Botticelli's *Venus*, above Venus; his brown blood splashed over Venus and the shell on which she's shyly standing."

David's eyes shone and he smiled. A bit of red lobster sauce was on his cheek. Dr. Fisher—Laura—lifted the crumpled white napkin from her lap and, wiping his cheek, whispered: "Incredible, isn't it?" She hadn't interrupted him until now. "You almost relish each graphic detail, don't you?"

She returned the greasy napkin to her silky evening dress. David, his cheek tingling, wondered whether the sauce would soak into her dress. What a peculiarity it is that good manners demand that you should wipe the grease from your lips, and then that you put the greasy napkin on your best clothes. Wouldn't it be cleaner to put the napkin on the table? He wiped his lips and folded the napkin neatly in a square.

"I guess I do. Life is strange; I expect death to be stranger. Anyway, I have an important question. Should I see his body before it's burnt to ashes and flung to the four winds?"

"What do you think? You have to decide." When he answered nothing but only stared at her feverishly, she continued: "It's risky. It might be something that will haunt you for the rest of your life. Or it might help you concretize your father being dead so that you can grieve it all out. Hard to tell. Depends on how much courage you have."

"That sounds like a challenge."

Nearly every night, David dreamed his father's emaciated body was floating in his room, blood spreading over the white head bandage and dripping onto green embers on the floor, with steam coming out of the ashes.

He began to drink heavily, put on weight, and was so inattentive at work that he was laid off. To top it off, Laura announced that she was moving to Stamford, Connecticut, where she would work for a hospital. David decided to follow her. He did not have enough money to afford the move and the high rent around Stamford. So he sold his Steinway piano, the dearest possession he had.

He used to dream of becoming another Glenn Gould, playing nothing but the divine harmonies of Bach. With highest recommendations for the master's program in piano performance at Juilliard, David had prepared his audition by smoking pot to soothe his nerves. It didn't work. Tense and paranoid, he sweated while performing Brahms's *Variations on a Theme of Paganini*; the keys kept sliding away from his cold fingers, and so did the lines of musical thoughts. Instead of the theme of Paganini, the recurring melody and voice in his head was Mick Jagger's "Sympathy for the Devil." He failed to qualify, and it was then that he decided to pursue the practical path of applied math, to become an accountant, dealing with numbers and machines and not with that pompous European geriatric inquisition, classical pianists.

After being laid off, David was unemployed for a year; he was in a sort of hibernation, except when he saw Dr. Laura Fisher, which made him liven up for several hours. He gave her presents: an Egyptian mummified cat, which he had stolen from his grandmother on her deathbed, and the first edition of *Doktor Faustus* by Thomas Mann in Gothic print.

Then David got an excellent job with Prudential Insurance in Stamford. The employment gave him an aura of self-confidence and success. He put on more weight, which on the surface didn't bother him (though it made his skin sweat so that he got in the habit of wiping his forehead with his jacket sleeves). He liked discussing his future with Laura. In ten years, he would be making more than a hundred grand a year. Then he would be able to relax, play the piano, and in a manly way support his wife so that she wouldn't have to work, but could chirp like a bird in a lush tree. In twenty years, with wise investments, he could retire and spend half the year in Katmandu, and the other half in

Stamford. In thirty years….She encouraged him to talk and did not make judgmental comments.

His new well-being, however, ran aground. Dr. Laura Fisher announced that she was moving again, this time to Tokyo to open a private practice for American businesspeople. She had family connections and many friends there; she could quickly establish her practice.

"But I won't be able to see you!" David exclaimed.

"We can stay in touch." Laura fidgeted in her armchair.

"I won't be able to find another therapist as good as you."

"Don't worry, you will. Unfortunately, the time's up." She stood up.

"Please, I'd just like to say something important—" He stammered, and she sat down again and crossed her legs. He tried to hide that he was staring at her legs. She uncrossed them, and crossed them again.

"Well?" she asked.

He looked at her beseechingly and said: "I could move to Tokyo. They need insurance too, with all those earthquakes and tsunamis."

"No, that would be too much. There's too much transference here. You have to be on your own. I cannot hold your hands."

He literally wanted to hold her hands. "So, you are just going to leave? It's so easy for you? After all we've been through."

"Don't be childish. I enjoyed working with you. I learned a lot. But now I must go!"

She stood up and walked past him. Her skirt brushed against his shirt in passing, with a spark of static electricity. She walked out of the office, opened the door to the corridor, and waited for him to leave. He stared at her radiant silhouette against the darkness of the corridor; her green feline eyes shone, fascinatingly elusive.

She was beyond him. He could not have her. He had humiliated himself. He had tried to appear strong, and he had tried to appear weaker than he was, he had tried to be real, he had tried to be fake. He hurried out of the office, cheeks flushed, and wished to kiss her naturally crimson lips—it would be so natural—but did not kiss them.

At home David drank a whole little barrel of Dinkelacker beer. It was the equivalent of two and a half six-packs in cute packaging, tasting like bitter honey. The neighbors played the stereo loudly; the bass shook the walls, and David resented it. His wife was not home yet though it was 11 p.m. Her violin rehearsals were supposed to be over at eight. *Well, let her. I don't care what she does.*

When she walked in, she laughed at him. "You are pathetic. Drunk again? Don't you know that each glass of booze is an invitation to the devil to be your companion? He might refuse one invitation, but not a dozen."

"Where did you get that pearl of peasant wisdom?"

"How can you drink so much? Don't you know you are too fat?"

"Too fat for what? I'm as I please."

"How can you be so stupid? Tomorrow you'll complain of a headache."

"Leave me alone."

"I thought I did. It's nearly twelve o'clock."

"Where were you?"

"I had a cup of coffee with the timpanist. It was fun. He has a crush on me."

"Really?"

"I like him too."

"So you want to leave me? Go ahead! I don't care!"

"I know."

"No, I care." He flung the freezer open and poured himself a shot of pepper vodka. "Just to cork up the beer."

"Just to cork up your mind, so you don't have to think."

"I've had enough of your smartass comments. All you do is criticize me."

"Since you don't have enough self-criticism, somebody's got to do it. And what good is your therapist? You pay her a hundred bucks an hour, and she doesn't criticize you, apparently. It's amazing that though you think only of yourself, you haven't discovered anything smarter to do than get wasted."

The next morning, David called in sick for the first time on the new job. Beatrice was away at the Sacred Art Music School, giving lessons to preschool children. David wondered whether she was lying to him and having an affair; he was jealous, imagining her making love to a stringy bachelor in a greasy concert suit and a pair of black socks with toenail holes. But the jealousy was only a background disharmony in the jarring melodies of his helpless longing for Laura.

David circled the phone like a bird of prey circling a rabbit far down on earth. Trembling, he grabbed the receiver and dialed. After two rings, the message machine was triggered: "I am unable to come to the phone right now, but if you leave your message with your phone number, I will call you as soon as I can." Beep—a tidy, economical, Japanese beep. He hung up. He called again in five minutes and hung up. He poured himself a glass of vodka. With the cold drink becoming warm in his blood, his confidence rose. He left a message.

"Please, you must see me. I need to see you. You don't know all about my past—you don't know what I am capable of. If you don't—I must see you."

The minute he lowered the phone he lifted it again, pressed the redial button, and said into the tape recorder: "I'm sorry about the message. That was a stupid thing to say."

He waited the whole morning for a return call. It did not come. He called her.

"Yes, what? You know that after a message like that, I cannot see you. You are right, I don't know all about you, I don't know what you are capable of. I don't like threats, so I won't see you again."

"I am sorry. I was desperate. I just cannot accept not seeing you at least one more time."

"All right, but a security guard will have to be present."

"Don't insult me. I didn't mean I'd do anything bad."

"Those are the terms. We have to sever this relationship. It's becoming destructive to you and a source of worry to me. So we are getting together one more time, only to make a transition to you standing up on your own."

He sniffled the tears in his nose.

David walked into the Stamford Professional Counseling building, stepping on a quiet carpet of a hazy color; he didn't know what one would call it. Lavender? Alabaster? Some name that only sophisticated women know. A receptionist smiled at him, a professional grimace that revealed her capped front teeth. Her thin blood-red lips drew a curtain over her teeth as soon as she realized they were exposed; the shyness of her mouth was perhaps a carryover from her ugly-teeth days. With her long red nails, she tapped on the switchboard phone, and in the somno-lent voice of an air hostess on a trans-Pacific flight she reported his presence to Dr. Fisher.

David walked past the receptionist and tucked his shirt under the belt. He tried to suck in his belly and walked self-consciously

and awkwardly, despite stepping firmly in his leather shoes with
rubber soles. He advanced past several closed doors of other psy-
chiatrists and counselors.

Hers was open.

"See, I trust you. We don't need the security guard. I know
you didn't really mean what you said." Laura smiled.

He closed the door. She stood up and opened it. "Let it stay
open. It's more airy that way."

"But why should the door stay open? Are you claustropho-
bic?"

"Yes, in a way."

David laughed. "But this is like a boy visiting a girl in a girls'
dormitory! The door must stay open during the date."

"Please keep your voice down." She sat closer to him so that
they could speak in soft voices. She crossed her legs. There was
a narrow damaged patch on her thin black stocking above her
knee; he wondered whose ragged nail had torn it—hers?

"I've brought you a present. A compact disc of Beethoven's
Triple Concerto."

"Oh, that's sweet of you, but I cannot accept presents. Presents are like investments, they form bonds." Her skirt slid back
as she gesticulated. Flushed, David leaned forward and put his
palm down on her knee. She jerked back and shouted: "Keep
your hands off me!"

He leaped to grab her around the waist. She delivered him a
sudden blow with her high heels, a karate kick, which took all
the air out of his chest. She ran out shouting for security guards.

When he regained his air, he shrieked like a lonely bull.
He grabbed the Gothic hardcover of *Doctor Faustus* and tore it
to shreds. Then he pushed down an entire bookshelf, tore the
phone out of the wall, and smashed it on the floor. He growled

as he tore through hardcovers one by one. He busied himself so when two policemen arrived.

"I guess you don't like to read, do you?" a pot-bellied cop said, looking around at the shredded books.

"No, I don't."

"I cannot say I blame you," the cop laughed. "But, young man, keep your voice down. These people out there, they are sort of soft, you know. It scares them; you are a big guy."

David did have the property of looking much larger in anger than he was otherwise. The cop put some chewing tobacco in his mouth, analyzing the mess. A mustached cop in the doorway said, "Let's handcuff him."

"No, he doesn't need that," the potbelly answered from his belly. Noticing how David stared at his tobacco, he offered him a pinch. David made a ball out of it and chewed. Now they all chewed tobacco like some sort of sacrament. Leaning over a soothing-beige garbage bin, they took turns spitting out yellow-green mush. It created a good feeling of camaraderie among them. The cops tapped David on the shoulder as one of their people, stuck with bookish intellectuals who had put him through a bad head trip. They escorted him to the car.

At a 7-Eleven, the potbelly bought him a pack of chewing tobacco, so he'd have something to chew on while in the psychiatric ward. David had his own room with a phone. His insurance company's insurance policy would cover eighty percent of the expenses. The remaining twenty percent, considering that he would have to spend at least a week in the hospital, would be a hefty sum. David spit tobacco through the window into the yard, fuming. The worst was that she humiliated him and that he would never see her again. He'd been told the hospital had looked for a therapist for him, but none were eager to work with violent people. The floor was guarded by two big guards who looked like bouncers at a discotheque.

David was not allowed to leave his floor, not even to take one flight of stairs to the first floor, where he could buy the *Globe* and the *Financial Times*. But he did not resent the limitation. For the first time in years, he felt calm. He mostly snoozed. This was his first vacation, so to speak, in three years.

His boss called. "David, what's the problem?"

"I'm in a detox center. I've been drinking too much lately."

"I sympathize. I went through the same thing several years ago, after my divorce. I'd had it bad. My liver was diseased. It's still weak. How's yours, do you have pains?"

"A little." David lied to keep the conversation sympathetic.

"Ah, a little *crise du foie*! You definitely better kick off the booze. You know what's the best thing for your liver? Lots of water. Drink it all the time, even when you are not thirsty. Pure spring water really takes away the poison."

"Actually, I've begun to drink a lot of water quite spontaneously."

"Good, you've got good instincts. We all miss you in the office. Keep your chin up!"

This was the first genuinely friendly conversation David had ever had with his boss. It was good to have nothing to hide. It all came out for everybody to see. He could sincerely rebuild his life now; the zero level to which he had fallen was a good turning point. But his obsession with his therapist gave him no peace. He demanded to see her. He claimed he would kill himself if she didn't see him just one more time. She left him a message through a psychiatrist that if he tried to get in touch with her again, he would be liable for all the damages in her office and would be criminally prosecuted. After reading the message, David hollered in his cell, banged on the door, spat on the wall.

His rib cage hurt where she had kicked him. He was sure the pain came from the kick, not from a swollen liver. He screamed that his rib was broken, that it was a bad idea to create Eve out of a rib, that he needed an X-ray. But all he got was more lithium.

Beatrice visited him. "Aren't you ashamed of yourself? Your behavior is obscene."

"Do you think I don't know that?"

"You must change or I will leave you. I've had enough of your psychiatry. You are addicted to therapy more than to beer. You better straighten out, go to AA meetings if you need to, but now it's either psychotherapy or me. An hour of good music will do you more good than a month of therapy. At least it won't do you any harm. We used to enjoy playing together so much, the Spring Sonata, the Kreutzer—and you sold the piano for this?"

She spoke forcefully. David's mouth hung open. She made sense. And she looked startlingly fresh with her lips forming a cheerful wave, like an M calligraphically drawn; her thin black eyebrows and long lashes gave her face clarity and tranquil beauty.

"Don't stare like that! Now you are listening to me. You are like a bull led around by the muzzle. Don't you have your own voice of reason to guide you?"

He now loved her throaty voice that came from her chest, from a wellspring of soul deep within, making him shiver as if he were waking up from hazy nightmares to a cool dawn and a beautiful landscape of two glacial lakes connected by a stream. The two lakes were he and his wife and the stream was their marriage; if one lake grew dry, the other would replenish it. He was being replenished even now. He smiled, daydreaming about some future time when his lake rose higher than hers, so he would be the one replenishing her.

"What's that idiotic smile on your face?" she demanded, laughing.

MY HAIRS STOOD UP

WE COULD LIVE MORE EASILY in the country, but we like to be where the excitement is. We have always wanted to be around humans, to be as close to them as possible, to be their pets.

We have failed. Humans prefer animals neither as bright nor as capable as we are, with the exception of a few unfixed cats. They keep every imaginable sort of worm, monkey, snake, and marine monster and still would not have us. Oh, some humans keep one variety of our species, guinea pigs. But guinea pigs are nothing more than an inferior breed, and they are treated well by humans because humans are fond of inferiority in others.

I have always admired humans. What intelligence, what perseverance, what industry! I cannot keep up with their technology these days. I used to be able to enjoy their greasy cogs—if you got hungry, you could always get by around oily machines. Now their machines are greaseless, inedible boxes.

Even such a simple thing as a snack is dangerous; much of the food that seems to have been casually left over is poison for us. When tired of cement, you used to be able to take a stroll in the park. Now, you must abstain from eating, and what fun is it to spend a sunny day in the park, starving? The streets are even worse: as soon as you are in the open, humans step on you, throw stones, iron, whatever they have in their front paws. Where did they get this urge to kill? Not even cats are like that. Actually, we are too tough for them. But humans kill and kill and it's never enough for them. They do it neither to feed themselves, nor to enjoy themselves. Killing disgusts them, and yet they take pride in the ingenuity with which they can destroy us. They hate us. I don't know how else to explain it. They think we are ugly, and yet they keep bulldogs, who are neither as intelligent nor as good-looking.

Speaking of similarities, I have concluded that humans are similar to us. Humans believe the same thing. Whenever they have questions about themselves, they seek answers with us. If their livers hurt, they test our livers. If their eyes go blind, they test our eyes. The assumption is that if something is harmful to us, it is harmful to them, and that if we don't understand something, they don't either. We are siblings, we and humans. They live in walls, so do we. They eat old, burnt food; they even intentionally rot foods in greasy water. I don't see any essential dissimilarities between us, except that humans are bigger and, therefore, live in bigger holes. Their world is merely our world magnified. And yet, instead of friendship, which we had sought for so long, they feel animosity. We must hide from them, and they need not hide from us, even though they fear us.

I am not exaggerating when I say that their lives are an antithesis to ours. If they cooperated with us, provided us with clean conditions, we would carry no diseases, and we would create miracles in science together. Of course, now that we are pushed and shoved underground, we run into many health hazards, but most of the diseases we contract come from humans, not the other way around.

I've had some adventures trying to enter one of their new buildings, each one hermetically sealed. You often have to go through sewage, which is risky business because the shit may just pour all over you. But you grin and bear it and let yourself be washed into a broader pipe where you can catch a breath and have another go. To avoid the avalanche, you never go up during the day or evening.

Once the water shot me up a vertical branch; I took the first horizontal turn and reached a narrower pipe. I thought there would never be an end to it, and my lungs were about to burst, when I was finally shot out of the water. There was poison packed in grated plastic, which gave me enough of a footing to jump out. I slid on the porcelain floor. I rushed to hide behind a smelly metal box, which growled and crunched ice. I tried to climb into the box, lured by the smells of dead fowl. It was too tall for me, and I was curious about other large cubicles.

It was one of those modern buildings where it's hard to bite your way through. I prefer the old ones of cement and wood. Biting through wood is very good for you: it keeps your jaws strong, sharpens your teeth, relaxes you, and cheers you up. We take turns on a project of occupying a building, making networks of holes as corridors. Wood spurs you on into artistic playfulness. Having crisscrossed hundreds of old buildings, I found this new one, though less to my liking, tremendously mysterious. Still, in a large space, the first thing I rushed to was a large old crate, stretching to the ceiling. The crate was filled with thin vertical papers bound by thick paper and cloth. I took a brief snooze, my twenty-first nap. I nap a lot and count time accordingly.

Sunlight woke me through a crack. I was surprised that the new building, nearly hermetically sealed, would have wooden boxes with cracks, but I've heard that humans grow sentimental and wish, as they go into the future, to be able to go into the past at the same time—that's greed for you. So they get all kinds of boxes from dead humans, who got the boxes from other dead humans, and the more generations a thing has lasted, the crazier humans are about it.

I peeked out of my crack. Several humans of varying sizes sat at a horizontal plank of wood on four sticks, and walked between the elevated plank of wood and a big white box where they keep winter. They cracked and sucked some eggs they had stolen from chickens, drank black steaming water from burnt beans, squealed and growled a bit, and then walked out of the cubic space.

I took a couple of bites from the bound paper just to play down my hunger. Maybe you could live on that paper; there must be something nutritious about it: probably those dark things running one after another in lines, looking like the droppings of flies. The lead-smelling shapes are squeezed into squares—a mark that humans have arranged them. I like the taste of leaded cellulose, though I am not exuberantly fond of paper.

Having grown certain nobody was in the large cubic hole, I crept out for a stroll. I didn't feel quite safe, as if something might hit me from behind, so I did my walking against the walls quickly, and actually, it must have looked more like running. Well, I admit it, I was kind of running.

I crawled into a white box, where they keep summer with the sun in zenith. Actually, it can be so hot in those boxes that I think they keep hell there. I crawled in through a hole against the wall, climbed through a narrow passage and to another hole into the centre cubicle, the baking chamber. It still smelled of various animals that had been broiled for human pleasure. It raises the hair on my tail to think how humans put innocent creatures into the gas chambers to burn them! After my tour through the hell box, I returned to the lead paper and took an intoxicating snooze.

The noise of humans woke me up. Through the crack, I saw one human opening the hell box and another sliding into it a metal board with a large animal carcass on it. I couldn't tell at first what animal it was—it had only two legs, without feet, sticking up, and it had no fur or feathers, and was much too large to be a chicken. I thought it could be an infant human. They gazed languidly at the carcass in the hell box. And then again, nothing, except smells of burning flesh. I spent a lot of time sniffing the lead on the paper, snoozing more than normal and not daring to leave the crate. Later on, humans gathered around the elevated plank and squatted on smaller planks of wood around it. With their front paws, they held up thin transparent stones filled with liquid, knocking them against each other and gazing longingly at each other, then gulped the pale liquid cautiously. Then they ate some grass. After a while, one of them opened the hell box. The smell of burning flesh ignited my adventurous bone. They pulled the flesh out and let it sit on top, then disappeared again.

I was not brave enough to leave my shelter right away. But when I sensed they would be gone for a while, I crept out of my shelter and climbed up to the flesh container. I worked my way through the heat into its center. Oh, Dracula, how hot it was there! I sneaked into the animal to protect myself from the heat. The inside of the animal was large and spacious—I could have easily lived in it with a whole family, scrabbling around in muddy wheat. What better than to have living space with edible walls! I was so groggy I couldn't move.

Only vaguely did I hear the people return. I was presently being rocked left and right and lifted up. I surmised that the board and the animal were being placed on the elevated plank of wood. The walls of the turkey—I had noticed atrophied wings on the side of the body and I had concluded it must be a turkey—shook, and I heard a dull sound. When streaks of light penetrated my chamber, I realized that the humans were tearing the flesh off the turkey with their long iron claws.

On one side, they reached the ribs. The tearing stopped. In trepidation I wondered whether they could see me as I could see them. I decided that from light one cannot see well into darkness, but from darkness one can see into light only too well. Through a narrow crack in the flimsy stomach lining, I saw one human, refracted and distorted, cutting streaks of light flesh and streaks of dark flesh, piercing it with metal claws, and lifting it into its mouth. The human shouted. I cannot tell the moods of humans from their faces. I don't think they have moods and emotions. I know they scream and squeal and grunt and hiss, and mostly, they rattle quite monotonously. It is a strange custom they have, to gurgle noise when they are more than one. Maybe they keep themselves at bay from each other by their constant noise, the way dogs keep away from each other by growling and cats by spitting. Well, if my supposition that they hate one another (in a cold, unemotional way) is true, then I don't understand why they gather in groups so often. And if they are alone, they have special boxes that rattle out similar noises, flickering with lights.

After making sounds with its throat, the human was quiet. It stretched its lips and showed its flat teeth. I don't know what they have teeth for, when they cut their food with artificial claws.

It was pleasantly warm, and I could begin to breathe without strain. I did not dare move enough to eat the flesh around me. All of a sudden, the human stood up and light flashed into my eyes from a large metal surface. The metal cut into the bird and more light poured into my shelter.

I knew there was no more time to hesitate. Lest I should be cut with the edge of the super-claw, I jumped out of the bird.

I staggered, weakened by having been in the heat for so long, blinded by light. But I didn't stay still. I jumped forward, for you mustn't stay still when humans are around. You must never underestimate these creatures. They are awkward and slow, but suddenly, puff, gotcha!.

To make a long story short, I leaped out of the bird. I landed in a warm container of squashed cranberries. There were many high-pitched sounds in the room. My heart skipped beats, but when it did beat, it made up for the missed ones; it beat frantically. I jumped over and over again. The white stone of squashed cranberries tipped over; I ran and jumped from the edge of the elevated plank of wood. I fell into the lap of a human with bare legs. Some humans wrap their legs and others leave their legs bare. The things they use for wrapping are soft and fun to chew; I heard they were mashed balls of cotton. Actually, I had never chewed their wrappings, and now I had no time to take up that experience as, at any rate, there was enough new experience pouring into my life, and I wanted to make sure that experience would not be my last.

I bounced off the lap, which was changing angles as the human fell to the floor. The chair squeaked and the human screamed. But I have already said there was a lot of screaming. I am repeating myself. They were repeating themselves too. I did not know why they screamed so much. I wished to think that it was all because of me, but I was too humble to dare to imagine that those powerful creatures that raised inedible buildings would have given little me so much recognition. Someone else fell on the floor—it was a furry floor but I couldn't figure out what sort of animal they had skinned for it—with a dull thud and a piercing shriek. A couple of humans were throwing their metal claws at me. I ran behind a white box.

Well, these humans were preoccupied enough. Some vomited right there on the floor, others over the elevated plank of wood and over the turkey. Then they took everything that was on the table and put it into dark plastic bags. What a pity that the half-digested food all went to waste. But I was not in the mood to try to save the food. First I wanted to save my stomach. I enjoyed seeing them walk out of the room in their usual vulnerable manner, on hind legs—when I used to love them, I worried they might trip any moment. Once they were gone, I scurried across the floor and slipped into a garbage bag, where I found the bird. I hid inside its walls once again; that was the only way I could think of escaping, knowing they would throw it out sooner or later.

I have just said "when I used to love them." Do I no longer love them? That's right. They are arrogant dirty bastards. Yet we have courage to eat what they eat, and to sniff what they sniff. On the other paw, they would not touch what we eat. I spent so much time liking them. I could not just like and like without encouragement to go on.

I hate them. The way they cut up some of us, the weakest among us, in their experiments and feed us poisons to see just how we'd take it, that is wicked. And how many times have they nearly killed me? I could have killed some of their old ones, but I haven't done it. Whenever I entered their cubicles and sniffed the air, I could tell whether there were old, feeble mammals there still breathing. I could have easily chewed their necks and bit through their jugulars; I was considerate and let them sleep on. It is true, though, that whenever I ran into some who didn't breathe, I began to tear their flesh, making the point that they were animals clean enough to eat. But look at how they treat us. They tear us apart while we are still alive, and when we are dead, they throw away our corpses without ever considering them edible, even though our flesh is more nutritious and richer in minerals than theirs.

Humans have repaid our kindness with hatred, our admiration with contempt, our service with poison, our love with murder. But we will outlast them.

CHARITY DEDUCTIONS

I HAD ALWAYS been proud to be an American, and I felt sorry for those who weren't Americans. Several years ago, as I watched the starvation in Ethiopia on CNN, I wanted to do something about it. I gave nine hundred bucks to one of those charity deals and then I read in the papers that the CEO got more than four hundred grand a year. I was upset—I was feeding his fat bum, plus paying his diet bills, instead of the people I was trying to feed. And then I read where the money sent to Ethiopia went: the Ethiopian government confiscated most of it to buy artillery from Russia and Slovakia in order to attack Eritrea again. I realized you can't do charity through an institution. The red tape is going to tie your hands, your money, and nothing—nothing good, that is—will be done.

So when the war in Bosnia dragged on, and predictably, international organizations helped it drag on, I grew exasperated. The U.N. created a safe haven of Srebrnica, and then disarmed the Muslims in it, and the Dutch soldiers helped the Serbs enter the disarmed city. Then the Serbs shot 8,000 men (mostly boys) in the soccer fields. And in Sarajevo, the food that was dropped by international aid organizations served mostly to keep people alive so Serbs would have live target practice. Out of contempt for relief organizations, I decided to help alone—privately. Our country is built on private enterprise, that's why it works. If charity is going to work, it too has to be private initiative—an individual helping an individual. I figure, if half the people in the world can't manage, the other half can help them, one on one, and there won't be any problems. When you have excess of blood, you donate some, and even your health improves. I believed in such beneficial sacrifice.

Of course, to be truthful, I'll say that the American system of tax deductions is the greatest source of philanthropy and big-heartedness in the world. If the tax laws had been written a little differently, we wouldn't worry about the misery in the world half as much. Nothing wrong with that. It's the results that matter, not the motives, and our country achieves wonderful results. Sometimes.

I went to a Bosnian refugee camp, looked around, and when I saw a miserable family—a thin, birdlike man, a woman in a scarf, and a sad-looking fifteen-year-old with big eyes—I said, I'm going to help them, provided they speak English. I don't have the time to learn other languages, and if people haven't learned English by now, in their adulthood, they probably won't. Only kids and secret agents really learn languages.

"You guys want to go to America?"

"That's my dream. I know it can't happen," said the woman.

"Yes, because it's far from all this," said the man and pointed at his surroundings.

"Yes, because of the NBA," said the kid. "My name is Toni, like Toni Kukoc."

They all looked intelligent, or that's the impression that their bulging eyes created since they reflected so much light. I had the impression their lights were all there, literally. I asked them what they did that they could speak English. The man said he was a chemical engineer. The woman was a high school teacher of sociology and geography. That struck me as funny—I mean, who'd want to study sociology and geography at high school, and then what good did it do? Is that what these people did—study sociology at high school? No wonder they went to war. And why would you want to study geography if you don't have enough money to travel? It's like studying wine from books without ever drinking anything but Avia and Concho y Toro. (By the way, that's what I drink. I just can't see pissing away more than ten bucks per day. Even ten bucks is disastrous, $3,650 a year, plus it's not tax deductible, and in terms of gross income, you need to make five and a half grand exclusively to afford that).

My not drinking lavishly actually allowed me to do the charity, which would be fully tax deductible—my airfare, their airfare, groceries for them, one quarter of my utility bills, since they would occupy roughly a quarter of our house. I could even make money on charity expenses: the expenses could sink me into the lower tax bracket. Yes, with some creativity, I could help this family and it wouldn't cost me a cent. I won't go so far as to say that if I were squarely in the middle of a tax bracket so that my charity deductions couldn't knock me down into a lower one, that I wouldn't consider this charity at some of my real expense, but I could see the beauty of it all. Rather than give money to the government to bomb away, I could do international goodwill, improve America's standing as a friendly and generous nation.

Anyway, the man was a Croat, the woman a Muslim, and the lad considered himself a Bosnian.

I worked out their papers, and was eager to get them on our rich diet as soon as possible. In Cincinnati, they got exile status, and for a while they'd stay at my house, until they got their feet on the ground. My wife May was all excited about helping them, and so was my daughter, Tina, who was sixteen. Our two older kids had already gone to college; one was finishing up at OU in Business Administration, and the other was trying to become a professional baseball player, now as a member of a farm team in Birmingham, Alabama. Anyhow, the two sons gone from our house made the house too large.

May and Tina welcomed us at Covington International Airport in Kentucky. We stopped by at Starbucks, and I got them Venti cappuccinos.

"So big?" commented Selma.

"Is that coffee?" Miro asked. "It tastes like hot chocolate and water."

As they were hungry, we went to Big Horn steakhouse. Free trips to the salad bar, eat as much as you like. Sixteen-ounce steak.

"This is beautiful," Miro said. "How can they just give that much meat?"

"You better get used to it," May said. "Everything here is big."

In the middle of the meal, Selma gasped. "Blood, I see blood!"

"Where?" I asked.

"Right here, in the steak. It's not cooked!"

"Oh, yes it is—it's just medium rare, juicy."

"In our country, we can't do that, we cook it all the way through," she said. She couldn't eat afterward and clearly fought down a gag.

They slept, it seemed, for two days, and when they woke up, I admit, what we did was not the most fun—we took them to our Unitarian Fellowship. The congregation, or rather fellowship, loved hearing about a Bosnian family. For a while, all of us were invited to dinners, to several prosperous homes of doctors and businessmen. But that lasted only about a month until the novelty of charity wore off.

No one in the family drove. "We didn't need to," Miro said. "In Sarajevo, you could walk everywhere or take a tram."

"Oh, we loved to walk," Selma explained. "Every night, half the city would be in the streets, walking back and forth, drinking coffee, chatting with friends in Bascarsija. You know, the old town that looks like a bit of Istanbul."

They seemed to consider this a mark of high culture—not to be able to drive because they came from such a fine cosmopolitan city, unlike faceless American suburbia. The consequence of this was that my wife and I gave them rides to Kroger's for their groceries, and then to the symphony hall to listen to Bruckner—they were amazed that I had no interest in the symphony. Actually, I enjoy something great, like Beethoven symphonies, but Bruckner? I don't have the time. Then, when I still worked as an accountant and had just begun to study the possibility of day trading, I worked seventy hours a week, and after seventy hours of high concentration, give me Mozart, something to relax me, something that's harmonious, not something that sounds like a thousand cats in heat—spayed cats in heat, spayed just a few days too late. Maybe I could have gotten into Bruckner if I didn't spend so much time driving them around. Maybe I would have even read Musil, *Mann ohne Eigenschaften*. That's what Miro read.

Plus, Toni needed to go to basketball practice. He got onto the high school team and wanted me to arrange for him to talk to UC Bearcats coach Huggins. "I don't know the guy," I said. "All I know is he's a horrible alcoholic and workaholic, and he abuses his team so much that they always start the season ranked number one but by the end of the season can barely walk—all bandaged up, if not hospitalized. If you are good enough, he'll learn about you, don't worry. They got scouts out there."

Yes, he was growing tall, but not the strong kind of tall—lanky, fragile. You feared watching him play that any minute he'd fall and break into pieces. Bearcats, who were known for their tough physical game, would tear him apart.

At least the boy had ambition, I have to admit that. More than could be said of his father. The only chemical engineering the man did was to smoke five packs a day and stink up the whole house. And the man made pathos-filled faces when he smoked, as though he was considering the fate of the solar system, which would vanish in five billion years. His mustache drooped, his eyebrows rose like his eyes didn't have enough space, and he looked at me like someone stepping into his dream, trampling on it. I know, I don't sound generous right now, but I need a valve to complain. Charity may be easy but generosity is hard. I mean, personal generosity. Giving money directly, even to a fat cat CEO, to handle the kind of moodiness in people that probably led to the wars would be much easier, but here I was, committed. I like to finish what I start, so even as my antipathy for the family grew, I thought I'd see them through it all, until they became gainfully employed citizens. But that smoke tested me. Nobody in my family smoked, but everybody in theirs did, even Toni the kid. His mom would shrug, lifting her lighter to the cigarette dangling from his lips. "Better that he do it with us than with gangsters outdoors."

"But how will he become a college basketball player if he weakens his lungs?" I said.

"He's not weakening anything, he's only smoking."

"No smoking is the rule in this house, as I am allergic to it."

"Allergic to smoke? Is there such an allergy?" Selma asked. "You Americans are very inventive when it comes to allergies."

"I just don't like it, all right? Do I have to explain? And don't you know about lung cancer?"

So during the day they would open the window and smoke, and the smoke would climb up through my window, and in the winter, they'd run up our heating bills. I don't know where they thought the heat came from, that it was like Iceland, or something, just coming up from the earth for free, and I bet it's not for free there either. At night, they thought I didn't know they smoked inside.

"In our country, everybody smokes." Milo spoke reproachfully, like it was an American shortcoming that we no longer collectively gassed ourselves.

"What country is it?" I couldn't abstain from asking. "Or rather, what country was it?"

They just looked at me pained and soulful. Was Bosnia a country? Yugoslavia? One wasn't recognized yet and the other had mostly fallen apart. Well, I could sympathize with them there. That's why I love America; we got this amazing country. Yes, smart people like that, they deserved better. But then, look at Tesla, he came from that part of the world, landed with a few cents in his pockets, and lit up the globe with his work and energy. And he didn't smoke, did he? The mysteries of motivation!

"What can we do when we worry so much? We must smoke," said the wife, and stretched her arms wide, unmindful of the fact that her shirt wasn't buttoned on top. She didn't wear a bra, another mark of European sophistication. I wondered what happened to her religion. She brought her arms back and said, "See, I don't know what to do with my hands without cigarettes."

I was copaying their health insurance, and Caritas was paying the remaining portion of it. I bet these guys figured that if something went wrong with their hearts, bingo, they would get a heart transplant, which, by the way, costs about $195,000, for free, and they could keep smoking until they'd get another heart,

lung, kidney. This is the country of replaceable parts. Many ex-
iles come here just for medical reasons; they land in NYC, rush
off to a city hospital and say, "Take care of me! You are rich and
I am poor, and you owe it to me." Yes, our medicine is the best,
no doubt about it. Of course, people go to Canada and Germany
for the same reasons.

But perhaps they were not thinking about it at all. That was
too pedestrian, pragmatic, crude for them. Their thoughts and
feelings were subtler. Ordinarily, smoking is a premeditated
murder, but this was simply meditational murder. Misapplied
eastern mysticism taking place via venomous breath.

"Yes, what can we do when we have to think about so many
things," said Milo. "We must smoke." He winked at me.

Did he see how Selma's breasts flashed at me? Did he mind?
Or was that normal to them? They had probably spent their
summers at nudist beaches on the Adriatic. Maybe he'd seen
it, and now wanted to relax me—Americans were notoriously
uptight when it came to sex, and he tried to relax me with his
charming wink.

There was one thing they liked to do in their worries: talk on
the phone. I told them they could do it now and then when the
news was bad. But they called up home at least twice a week—
Tuzla, Belgrade, Zagreb—and the bill was horrendous.

(They were actually from Tuzla. Later I found out that Tuzla
hardly had any war. They had that explosion in the center that
killed seventy people, and a casualty here and there, but basically,
the city had stayed out of the war. In other words, they were safer
there than they would have been in downtown Cincinnati. I wish
I could have helped someone from Srebrnica or Bihac or some other town where people were truly hopeless. But never mind now.)

"The phone is very expensive," I said.

"Oh, is it? I read how you could hook up through the Internet and make free international calls."

"I doubt it, my friend. Nothing is for free."

"We better look into it. It will benefit you as well," Milo said.

"That's a good idea. Let's turn on the computer and find out."

Milo sat next to me, and I breathed shallow because he reeked of nicotine, old wet nicotine, maybe decades of nicotine coming out of his pores. I don't think you can get rid of that smell. We went to all sorts of sites. We followed the directions, but it didn't work, and then there were sites that guaranteed it would work, for forty cents a minute. But at that point, the man had already lost interest. He went down to my basement to use the weight room. He wanted to stay in shape. He'd stand in front of the mirror, sideways, an unlit cigarette on his lips, looking like a French actor, the kind that wears white socks, and scrutinize his biceps.

After all this, he continued to call freely as though we had transferred to the Internet, but the fact was that it cost 89 cents a minute, and that with a $4.95 a month international calling plan.

I bought them a used Nissan so they could get around on their own. May and I taught them how to drive. Selma learned most quickly. After she got the license, she said, "I just wanted to see whether I could do it. I can. But I don't really want to drive. It's too dangerous, too expensive, a bad habit, really. I don't trust myself, and how could I trust others on the road? Someone may fall asleep, or have a stroke and slam straight into my car. All these ninety-nine-year-olds driving terrify me. The road is as dangerous as a low-grade civil war."

True, wherever I drove her, she trembled in the backseat— wouldn't sit in the front, for she'd read it wasn't safe—and she'd bite her nails. So I was like her driver, driving her even to the mosque, made out of thick concrete, along the highway toward Dayton. (A propos of Dayton, even though the Dayton peace accord had already been implemented, Selma claimed they could not go back yet; they would not be safe.)

Now that she learned how to drive, she gave me tips from the back. "Why go through yellow lights? Can you cross the double yellow line?"

I can understand post-traumatic stress syndrome, but this was more like pre-traumatic stress syndrome. If clouds came, she'd sigh. "Oh my God, are these tornado clouds?"

"I have no idea."

"Isn't this tornado country?"

"Sure. Tornados, torpedos, tomahawks, we got it all."

"But the house is made of wood. In our country, they make them of brick."

I didn't say anything. She'd want us probably to rebuild the house, and make it of stone, so they'd feel safer, like back home. Or maybe this was her version of nostalgia. She dreamed of their beautiful redbrick, red-roof homes. (Like nearly all the Europeans I met, these guys considered everything European superior to anything American, starting from their customs and produce and doorknobs and ending with the soul—we Americans are superficial and they are deep and passionate. If their countries are so fine, why don't they use their own money, not ours?)

I don't think people that get scared that easy should have wars, that's just my opinion. Maybe Swedes should have wars, if they are all like Borg and that other guy, the tennis player, Edberg, who don't get scared under pressure. But Swedes, just as if to spite their potential, don't participate in wars. Neutral, pacifist. Or Jamaicans should have major wars. They are too relaxed for something like that. I know, these are stereotypes and as such probably all false, but it's the nervous devils, like these Balkan peoples, who get into wars, simply because they are least suited for them. What you fear is what you get.

They always worried about their relatives, or so they said, but it turned out all the relatives survived. Now, I don't doubt that a hundred thousand people were killed in the war and a hundred thousand disappeared (many to reappear in the States, Germany, and Saudi Arabia), but the rest of the four million survived, and not only that, but turned out to be profiteers. Many people used the misery of those two hundred thousand as a boon to get international sympathy, green cards, royal treatment all over the world. Maybe the non-victim types schemed to have the war, knew it was coming, could run away in time and show pictures of those who couldn't. Their economy didn't work before the war. They couldn't emigrate. The war comes; half of them emigrate. And their economy back there is even worse than during the war. You know, I am not xenophobic, but I believe in the concept of home. Stay home. Visit briefly. Go home. Don't attack anyone, don't invade. When attacked, don't run away. Very simple rules. The world would be much better off if people followed them.

I inquired at Proctor and Gamble to get Miro the engineer an interview. When I finally arranged it, Miro was indisposed; he claimed he had food poisoning, and gave me a lecture about how chicken should always be thoroughly cooked, especially if you're feeding people from another continent who have grown up with a different set of bacteria. When I wanted to reschedule the interview, he said I should postpone it for a year, until his English got better.

"Isn't chemistry spoken in the language of formulae?" I said. "You don't need much English. You can visit with me and see that there are Chinese chemists who speak hardly any English, but they are the movers and shakers in the company anyway because they are geniuses in the language of chemistry."

"That may be true, but my chemical engineering is ancient— old socialist backward science. I should read some current chemistry to catch up."

I got him the books that were used in chemical engineering at U.C., but those books stayed unopened.

Instead, Miro went downtown, set up a table to play chess at the Fountain square, and hustled for money. He was good at speed chess—that just proves the point, that he was smart and had no excuse not to be productive—so he made some money, but whatever he made he spent at the racetrack, where once a month May took him with Selma. He was not good at betting. He had the theory that the thinnest horses always won. I don't know why he had that theory; he himself was getting fatter. The American food clearly agreed with him, so much so that he ate all the time. I don't think he saw himself as exploitative. He thought he was repaying us by his genius; he volunteered to teach Tina how to play chess, and strangely enough, she liked it. Every evening before going to bed, she played a few games with him, and he complimented her on how quickly she was learning. She laughed at many moves. First they played at the kitchen table, but later, on the floor, sprawled sideways, on elbows, like Romans at dinner. I knew of course that Tina was smart, and for a while, May and I thought it was wonderful that she was getting into chess. Chess at seventeen—there could be many worse ways to spend evenings. At least that kept her off the phone and out of the bathroom.

Toni did not like to play chess. "That's for nerds," he said. "It makes me too nervous. A basketball player must have good nerves and good posture." I did not pay much attention to the whole thing. I thought it was a waste of time, except for keeping adolescents out of trouble and retirees from getting strokes. (For retirement, maybe I'd learn how to play the game if it weren't for online investing. I think trading stocks will do for my synapses. On the other hand, who knows whether there will be a stock market in thirty years? Maybe computers will make it obsolete the way they are making chess simply an antique game, and all the profits will go to IBM and Microsoft.) Anyhow, the little chess tutorials certainly did not compensate for the amount of food our guests ate.

At first during meals, Miro and Selma, but not Toni, were demure and dainty. They ate little and declined seconds, and kept saying, "Oh, it's so kind of you. How will we ever be able to repay you?"

But then, when they thought we were asleep, they'd tiptoe to the refrigerator and raid it—drink a quart of milk in one standing, straight from the carton. They'd eat all the salami, roast beef, and even uncooked Frankfurters. I thought the war had something to do with religion—no true Muslim would have eaten the stuff in the refrigerator, certainly not the ham, but Selma did not pay attention to the subtleties.

When I saw them eating at the refrigerator, the whole family, she said, "We're still having jet lag, that's why we are hungry at four in the morning. That's almost noon in Bosnia, time for dinner."

The first time this happened, I laughed. But I never knew anybody to have jet lag for more than a month. Even a year later, they'd have their feast at four in the morning, eating by the light of the refrigerator.

All these matters so far were a prelude for a clash. Since I am not a very subtle guy, I imagined my moods made them un-comfortable as well, and here we were, the donor and the donee, passing through the kitchen with many knives. One of these days we might use them.

Now, my daughter actually liked them. When Tina got her driver's license, she drove them wherever they wanted. She was proud of them. I was worried that their son would take up with her. She was only a few months older than he, and I could catch him staring at her. Naturally, as a father, I have trained myself not to look at my daughter's body, but I am aware of it, in a sort of protective way, and I know it looks good. So I had to make sure that the two would not stay in the house alone.

But one Monday at breakfast, when we were to eat togeth-er—May's idea, to have lavish Monday breakfasts to start the week in a good mood—we realized we hadn't all gathered.

"Where is Miro?" asked Selma. "Where could he have gone?"

"He's still probably asleep," May said.

"How would you know?" Selma said.

I wanted to get breakfast over with fast so I could read thes-treet.com and realmoney.com before the market opened at 9:30. I had put thirty thousand dollars in one stock, Zenith, since I'd read they had developed a high-resolution screen for TV, and the stock was supposed to fly that Monday with the licensing ap-proval. Generally, I held no positions over the weekend, but here, this seemed a sure bet. Still, I was nervous, wondering whether the stock would double or triple. I could make a yearly income in an hour! So the last thing I wanted to worry about was Miro's sleeping habits.

"He's an early riser," Selma insisted. "Where is he?"

Tina was not there either, but I assumed she was preening in the bathroom. So we ate hash browns, which my wife liked to prepare her way, with sesame oil and anchovies and CFO eggs. While enjoying the taste, I tuned out of the crisis conversation—I enjoy nothing more than orange yolk and crispy hash browns my wife's way.

"Maybe she took him to a grocery store to buy cigarettes?" May said, when Tina was nowhere to be found. They all wanted me to call the police and to drive Fountain Square to see whether the two were chess hustling together. So I drove, but I did not find them at the Square. I was worried, too, worried enough that I forgot to check my stock until noon. But on the way back, it suddenly occurred to me how naïve I had been. Would the multibillion-dollar industry allow for high-resolution TVs to put them out of business or to put them at a disadvantage? I rushed home, through red lights, and ignored May and Selma. By the time I had logged on, it was too late. Zenith had not gotten approval, and the stock crashed. My thirty thousand had turned into five thousand in a couple of hours.

In dismay, I sold my whole position. The stock bounced to ten thousand on a rumor that it would get approval after all. I bought back, and the stock fell again just as my wife shouted at me to clear off the lines. So now I had lost more than thirty thousand, and I was so distraught that I couldn't worry about Tina and Miro. I was so stunned that I couldn't talk about it to May, and she screamed at me that I was a cold beast not to be out looking for our daughter.

The whole day passed, and not a word from them.

Did he kidnap her? Did he want ransom? How much would he want? Bastard, that's probably what he's up to, I thought. The gall of it! First he distracts me so I lose money, and then he'll want money from me.

We kept calling the police. We waited in trepidation all night, all of us, dreading the phone ringing. What if we got a report that he'd killed her? That they were both dead in a big car crash?

But there was no call. There was an email from Tina, however. She said, *Sorry Mom and Dad, Miro and I fell in love and we could not help it. He's such a wonderful man, and we have so much in common. Maybe we'll be back in a month, but maybe not, maybe in a year, who knows? We are incredibly happy, and we love you all.* Miro wrote something in Bosnian to his family. Selma was devastated. We all were, except for the boy, who did not seem to care.

I wish I could go on and say exactly what happened, but this brings us up to date. Where are they? What to do next? Go on the road? Distract myself by investing in Cisco? I have no idea. I am going out of my mind. When this is all over, I swear, no more generosity. Not from me. Well, maybe I'd donate to the military. I have just put 20K into Raytheon. I think considering our love of bombing, the missile producer will triple in value if we get another war...no ifs, only whens. This time, I'd like an honest, old-fashioned war. An invasion of the Balkans would be good. Tony Blair is suggesting it now, during the Kosovo crisis, and I'd say, let's do it, but not in order to help anybody.

Everything is evaporating—my family, my money. And it's early April. Tax time. Both fool and tax time. Only fools pay taxes anyway. Why should I pay any taxes? I have paid more than enough.

A TASTE OF THE SEA

NEAR MY HOMETOWN there was no large surface of water. We were surrounded by forests; wherever you turned it was green, but there were not even any small rivers to give you refreshment.

One summer, our father announced he would take our whole family to the seacoast, my ten-year-old sister, eight-year-old brother, and six-year-old me. We boarded the old grey Mercedes coupe of my father, an old beat-up ambulance, which he had bought after it stalled on the way to the hospital, with him as the emergency patient in a kidney-stone crisis. Our father hadn't even scraped the red cross from the windows; he said it helped in traffic, and you couldn't see much out of the car because the windows were not transparent, except in the front. Still, in the paint there were cracks through which I stared at revolving fields as I sat on the little sideways paramedic's seat.

After Zagreb, in the mountains, the engine was overheated. We made frequent stops to fill the engine with water, but to no avail, the car smoked like a steam engine. And then, in a steep town with tall firs and large vistas, and cool air, the car would not move, completely stalled. As failed nomads, we abandoned all hope of reaching the sea or home, and I suggested that we settle right there in the town, because I hadn't seen a more beautiful one yet; the mountains were taller than around our town, so the town was bound to be better. My mother bopped me on the head to shut me up, while our father spoke beneath his bristly moustache in a highly unbiblical vernacular and tried to fit a new part into the engine, a part which looked like a heart with a bunch of black veins and white arteries branching out of it. When the sky changed from purple to indigo, our father managed to turn the engine on by rotating a hook which was stuck in the engine, and white smoke came out in the back. I crawled on all fours to smell it, because there is nothing more intoxicating than gasoline exhaust, the smell of progress itself. We went on, up a sinuous road, past waterfalls and scraggly evergreen trees. At midnight we were atop a bare mountain, gazing into the distance. "The mountain is bare because the Venetians cut down all the trees, so the wind and rain washed off all the soil; and Venice is down there, over the sea, on the other side, floating on rotting wood," said our father.

"Where's the sea?" I asked.

"Down there. If it were daytime, we could probably see it."

We drove down serpentine roads, and I fell asleep. We reached the coast and I was still asleep, and it turned out I was not the only one. All of us were, including the driver, our father. We were woken when the car hit a hanging tree branch at a precipice. My father quickly stopped the car. We all got out and stared down the precipice. The drop ended in the blackness of the sea, and roaring waves crashed against the rocks. "Wow, we could have been dead," I was shouting. "That's exciting!"

I was amazed that our father had lapsed, made an error, for I had considered him infallible. Father said, "God saved us. He let that olive tree branch hang low, so it would hit the car and wake me up before I drove over the edge."

"Really?" I asked. "He saw our car and bent the tree in a couple of seconds so we'd hit it?"

When we reached the sea's level, I begged, "Let's stop, I want to see whether it's salty."

"It is. Be patient till we reach Zadar."

But I insisted, and my brother and sister joined in. I had not believed that the sea was salty, because where would they get so much salt? When it was thought that the Russians were about to occupy Yugoslavia, we couldn't even get a kilo of salt in the shops, so how could there be enough salt for the whole sea?

Our father did stop. We took off our shoes as if about to step on a holy carpet, and together we walked into the water. I caught some water into my palms and drank it. "Wow, it is, it is!" I shouted. In the black distance of the ocean there were lights of fishing boats. A cool breeze came from the water, the waves crept up the sand, and hissed or rather whispered and murmured like a huge yet benevolent monster.

We camped outside Zadar in a used tent that our father had bought from an army doctor.

On the first morning we three kids leaped into the water on an air raft. I couldn't swim, and my sister told me she would teach me how, but not yet, because she was too busy enjoying herself. We were rowing with our hands and pushing each other for space. The sun scorched our backs, and we sprinkled cool water over our bodies; when the water dried, we had salt on us, and we licked it from each other's skin like a family of cats.

Suddenly, in the middle of the marine delights, I slipped off the raft. The cold water cut my breath, and I sank beneath the surface. I was surprised that I was not panicking and that it was taking place all so slowly. Above, through my cold eyes, glared the enormous light blue green with a shadow in it, the raft which was just out of my reach, farther and farther above me. The shimmering surface of the water was like melted lead, which I had melted from stolen lead pipes and poured into cups. The shimmering was vanishing and reappearing. What a beautiful sight, I thought, and now in it, you will drown. Somehow I could not believe it, that I would drown and die, because I was suspended in the water, in a gravity-proof state. The glittering surface above me seemed unreal, and whatever was beyond it was bound to be even more so, distorted and vanishing in the kaleidoscope of light.

Upon hitting the sandy bottom of the sea, I sprang up, ascending slowly, surprised at the gentleness of all my motion despite putting all the force I could in it. My fingers reached the raft, caught the edge of it, and I pulled myself out of the water with the help of my brother, who grabbed me by my hair, and my sister, by one arm. Only upon getting out of the water, as if fully realizing that I could have drowned, I grew scared. My nose was sore, my sinuses were sore, my ears hurt, I had a headache, and I began to moan, and then to laugh, water leaking out of my nose and ears.

In a night and a day, I had already twice been close to death, and I bragged about it, imagining I had grown, had become brave. I bragged to everybody that I had nearly drowned, though my brother and sister begged me not to tell our parents.

In the afternoon, I accompanied my mother and sister to shop. In the harbor was a large ship with three masts and sails. The sailors on the ship seemed to me to be pirates. I begged them to let me on the ship. They laughed and said, "What the hell. Madam, we'll entertain your son." And they took me aboard as if I were a toy, while my mother and sister shopped. One sailor, who was weightlifting, offered me to join him. I could not move the weights, except the smallest one that he used for one-arm exercises. The engine was switched on, and the ship let water out on the sides, the way I had out of my ears after the near drowning.

The sailors carried me into the body of the ship and told me we were below the surface of the water. "The ship goes four meters beneath the surface," a sailor told me.

My mother and sister came to pick me up, and I screamed, saying I did not want to go with them, but the sailors were traitors and handed me over. Soon we were in the tent. My mother and sister were unpacking eggs, vegetables, and meat while I talked about the wonders of the ship, and then I shut up, lost in thoughts about the engine, the masts. When my sister said something, I didn't listen to her. All I heard was the end of it: "We had to wait for an hour; it was so long, at least five meters long."

"Yes, very big!" I exclaimed. "It goes five meters deep into the water."

Everybody burst into laughter, while I was astonished that such an important and impressive fact was treated so lightly. I said, "What's funny? It did sink into the water five meters, the sailors told me."

"We were talking about the line in front of the butcher's, how long it was, and you say, yes, so big that it sunk into the water five meters! The whole line of people would have drowned!"

"It's not my fault," I cried, indignant, "that you care more about shops than ships!"

After a couple of weeks, I began to complain: "I want to go home, the sand here is no good; I can make better cities out of our sawdust!" And my brother joined me, saying he could not play Robin Hood on the rocky terrain, he needed a forest. Our sister wanted to stay; she collected pink starfish and shells. And our mother said that she should take care of the garden, which must be a mess by now. And our father said he was tired of all the salt, he felt like a smoked and salted ham and all he wanted to do for a week would be to lie in the shade of large dank oaks. And so we went home, and moved with joy into our previously scorned and now beloved woods.

.

FRITZ: A FABLE

Lipik, Croatia
1991

FRITZ, a gray German shepherd, who in his pointed face and thick tail resembled a wolf, howled so terribly that his owner, Igor Lovrak, went into his larder, greased his great-grandfather's rifle, and thumbed gun powder and bullets into the barrels before he dared to walk out into the yard. And even then he trembled, expecting bears or a band of thieves to be closing in. Just when Igor stumbled out in his wooden clogs, Fritz leaped so violently that he tore from the ground the thick pipe to which he was chained, and with a terrible din jumped over a hedge. A cat leaped onto the lamppost, barely escaping the dog, and climbed to the tilted and capped light bulb, and placed its paws over the lamp hook. Once settled, the cat didn't move.

Although usually obedient, Fritz wouldn't listen to Igor's shouts to stop. Igor, who was built like a weightlifter, dragged him by the chain, but almost all the ground he had gained he lost with Fritz's leaping toward the aloof enemy.

Igor locked him in the basement—Fritz knew how to open unlocked doors—but that didn't prevent Fritz from howling most unpoetically his ugly song all night. Igor couldn't sleep. He marveled at Fritz's voice box. After so many bullets of wind from the lungs into the vocal cords, you'd expect the cords to snap. Igor's nerves did, so he took up his ancestral gun and walked to the basement. His frizzy-haired wife, Dara, who couldn't sleep either, stopped him.

"Leave that gun alone. What good could you do with it?"

"Shoot the devil."

"Once the cat goes, he'll be all right."

"Are you suggesting that I shoot the cat?"

They sat up on the edge of their bed with their feet on the cold cement floor. It was past twilight. Against the paling sky, the lamp post appeared stark black. On the post was the silhouetted cat, in the same position as the evening before.

"The damned cat hasn't moved at all," said Igor.

"Are you sure it's alive?"

"Maybe it died of fright. Cats are such cowards—probably most of them die of heart attacks."

"I wouldn't call this cowardly. Maybe he's got himself electrocuted in the wires."

In the slanted, streaking sunlight, frosted branches of the hedges sparkled; in the hills, barks of beeches glistened. Loud sighing and intermittent snoring came from below, through the drains in the bathroom and the kitchen. When Igor turned on the faucet, even the water seemed to flow with the sleepy sorrow of a groaning hunter—or Igor's ears still murmured in the aftermath of the howling. Now he couldn't stay alert, although he had to go to work as a plumber at the spa hotels, where ladies from all over Croatia and Hungary came to improve their complexions in iodine mineral water. They languidly coiled in pink oval marble pools, and when adjusting pipes, he sometimes caught a glimpse of them—born-again embryos in halved and steaming eggs with ossified shells. Now he thought that if he wasn't alert at work, he might cause some damage, cut his fingers off.

Igor walked out and called the cat, but the cat didn't move. Its turquoise eyes glowed independent of the sunlight.

Igor whistled like a bird, but the cat's ears stayed unmoved. He didn't want to let the cat remain suspended dead above his house. If a cat crossing your path spelled bad luck, a cat crossing your wires and looming lifeless in your window spelled doom. Would crows eat the cat? Maybe pigeons? Owls? He got a ladder and climbed, shakily, up the cracked post that smelled of oil and tar.

When he reached for the cat, in a sudden blur the cat's claws and teeth lashed at his stretched hand. He lost his balance, dropped the cat, and gripped the post. After the cat, his ladder fell. Slowly, hugging the post, with splinters needling his palms, he descended to the ground. The claw swipes had made the back of his hand look like a fragmented music sheet, brown with age, and two bloody canine marks coagulated, captured, and for now silenced two disharmonious notes of fear and hate—but the notes kept the frequency of the song that sooner or later would find throats to grip.

"What happened to the cat?" Dara asked.

"That interests you more than what happened to me?" Igor poured plum brandy over the music sheet that the back of his hand had become, wincing at the wet melody of scorching pain his nerves were hearing. He pinched splinters from his palms. The splinters hadn't provoked a flow of blood while under his skin, but once they were removed, blood flashed in the emptied lines like comets in the sky.

"Well, that'll teach you to pick up a strange cat without gloves. Where is it now? It must be starving."

"I'll go get the dog and let him run after the cat."

"Let him stay down there—I'll feed the cat."

She walked out. Igor, pouring plum brandy down his throat, saw a gorgeous tabby with thick black stripes—a veritable black and gray picture of a tiger—scratching its back against Dara's thin ankles, which were in thick woolen socks. Her heels, he noticed, even now formed a dancer's right angle; she never forgave him for living in the provinces where she couldn't become a professional dancer. The cat lapped milk, rubbed his back against the socks, and its tail went straight up and grew fluffy, perhaps from the static that flared up from the socks. The tail tip waved joyfully above round testes. Dara picked him up, scratched his tummy, and the cat licked her palm and put his paw pads on her cheek. And so they stayed for a whole minute, gazing at each other with an interspecies sympathy.

"That cat's so thin," Dara said as she poured milk into a teacup. "We should take care of him."

"Is that up to us to decide?"

"Fritz will just have to get used to it. When he realizes that Bobo is here to stay, he'll accept and love him."

But Fritz couldn't get used to it. At night he barked mercilessly. He chased the cat up roof pipes and into the hills. Once, when the cat fled onto a thin birch, Fritz peeled the layers of bark with his teeth and then gnawed on the wood, like a beaver, until the tree fell. The flying cat barely touched the ground before it bounced over the dog and up a huge beech. Fritz dug at the beech roots and tore them, perhaps with the design to bring down that tree, too. And maybe after a month of labor he would have succeeded, if Igor hadn't found him and chained him again. Fritz's hatred for the cat grew legendary.

(And so, this story could have started like this: In a spa town there lived two mortal enemies, a cat and a dog. Now this was not unusual—there were many cats and dogs in the town, and they were all mortal and the hatred between them frequently entertained the inhabitants, Serbs and Croats, and the laughter of the inhabitants was loud. However, the hatred between most of the cats and dogs was amateurish compared with the hatred of a gray German shepherd and a gray tabby. The night the tabby appeared in the hedges on the edge of the town, the dog howled so terribly that his owner went into his larder and oiled his grandfather's gunpowder rifle....Anyhow, the story didn't start—nor will it end—this way.)

Fritz chased Bobo all over the hills and up many trees; and yet, when he dragged his feet home exhausted and disenchanted, unable to lift his hanging tongue into his mouth, he'd see Bobo strutting across the yard to his bowl of milk in the old barn's rafters. Once, after a day of chasing, Fritz fell asleep, and Bobo came up and cuddled with him. Bobo licked his nose, purred in his ear, then left. Pretty soon Fritz awoke with a howl; he sniffed himself all over and even bit himself trying to get rid of the odious odor, sucking and chewing his fur as though he'd been infected with cat flies.

Once, in a corner, Fritz surprised Bobo, who had been absorbed in the joys of tossing a dying mouse over his head. He flew at Bobo with predatory certainty. Bobo flew even faster past his face and tore his ear. Before Fritz had time to understand what had happened, Bobo was up on the wall, ostentatiously ignoring him. Fritz would have a vee cut in his ear for the rest of his life.

The inability of the two beasts to get along complicated the Lovraks' lives. They slept poorly. Fritz had been a passionate hunter even before Bobo showed up. He had leaped on anything that moved. But nothing matched this monomania for the cat.

"He hates life," Dara joked.

It was a miracle that the cat did not seek another home; but, as theirs was the outermost house in town, this may have been his last chance.

Who knows how much longer this would have been going on if people hadn't begun to behave like—and worse than—cats and dogs. Lipik was one of the first towns to be surrounded by the Serb armies. When rumors of approaching Chetniks with bared knives reached the town, and even more concretely, when a mortar shell shattered their roof tiles, the Lovraks rushed to get away. They couldn't find Fritz and Bobo to take them along— and besides, how could you take such two enemies in one little car? Many cars, tractors, and trucks drove out of town—Croats north to Bjelovar, Serbs south to Banja Luka.

Igor and Dara stayed in a basement belonging to Igor's brother in Bjelovar. Igor feared to walk out into the streets, lest he should be drafted and forced to run at Serb tanks armed only with a rifle. His sense of masculinity was insulted, for he saw himself as a brave man. In his youth he had been a bar fighter. That was how he had met Dara, when she worked as a tavern waitress. A giant drunk had stalked her and, when she finished her shift, attempted to rape her. Igor jumped at the giant and nearly strangled him. Dara had been grateful, and he had been proud. And now he was reduced to living with a bunch of onions and potatoes that in the winter sprouted their offspring; out of the old, shriveling fruits of the earth grew new pristine lives. And what could grow out of him?

He tried to do some good—he fixed all the plumbing and rewired the house—but once he was done, out of his bleak moods sprouted only cynicism, which Dara couldn't take for long. She abhorred the fact that Serbs were attacking, but she also detested listening to the venom Croats, including Igor,

spewed at the Serbs, as she was one. When Croatian bands began to burn out the houses of the Serbs who had left, she boarded a train to Hungary. Weeks later she sent Igor a card from
Belgrade, telling him that she hadn't felt safe in Croatia.

He was enraged. He had worried about her for weeks, and
now she didn't feel safe! And who was responsible for that, if
not the Serbs in Belgrade, whom she now served, cooking bean
stews in fast food dives, feeding former murderers and future
murderers? He read the card while watching pictures of Lipik in
the newsreel.

During the war, only a dozen elderly people remained in Lipik. Serb soldiers lobbed mortar shells into the town for weeks
without a break. Croatian policemen—there was no Croatian
army at first—defended the town, entrenched in the schools,
churches, and hospitals.

In the old Austrian spa buildings, targeted many times,
now loomed large holes, so that the ruins looked like skulls
with empty eye sockets, bricks and tiles strewn around like
broken teeth. Many tree trunks, cut in half from stray howitzer
hits, resembled the broken legs of tubercular patients, their yellow bones sticking out of crusty skins; the rest of the patients'
bodies, which should have been above the broken femurs, was
missing; the bodies may have hid in iodine vapors or slid into
the ground under the moss. Shards of stained glass windows
with peeing angels lay in the gardens and in pastel-blue tiled
swimming pools. The shards sank in a heap of dead crows and
the leaves of weeping willows.

The gloom notwithstanding, most people could take care of
themselves. At least they could run; they understood what was
going on. But how were animals to understand war? They trembled as though a natural calamity were taking place—thunder,

earthquake, fires. And all of these were taking place. A Lippizan-
er stable (from which Lipik got its name)—where for more than
a century one of the original lines of the Austrian white horse
was bred—had been firebombed. A white horse was seen running into the hills, its mane and tail and penis ablaze. Another
stepped on a cluster of mines and flew into the sky as a geyser of
blood, iron, and hooves.

When that Christmas Eve Croatian soldiers broke the siege and
took over the town, several of them wanted to enter the Lovraks'
house. But on the threshold stood a wolf-like dog, and next to the
dog, a tabby. The dog's paw gently and protectively lay over the
tabby's shoulders. When the soldiers came closer, the dog growled
most threateningly and the cat arched his back and hissed. The
soldiers, who otherwise might not have felt any qualms at shooting an inimical dog, were touched. They didn't insist on entering
the house, even though that may have been imprudent—Serb
snipers could have crouched in there, but the captain of the unit
decided that was highly unlikely, for the house had a large tank
hole gouged into its middle. On the way out, the Serb tanks had
blasted holes in many houses, according to the dog in the manger
fable: *if we can't have this, neither will you.*

Much later, when Igor returned, Fritz wouldn't let him into
the house.

"Don't you know me?" Igor shouted. "I'm your master."

But Fritz didn't acknowledge him. And when Igor wanted to
pet Bobo, who showed no resentment but a great deal of indif-
ference, Fritz growled jealously and nearly bit Igor's hand. Igor
backed off, and Fritz washed Bobo with his tongue.

With the help of the United Nations, Igor built a cabin in his
yard. He was lonely. Not even his dog liked him. Not even the
cat did.

He took photographs of Fritz and Bobo and captured the images of the two souls cuddling. Igor sent the pictures to his wife in Belgrade. He wrote a letter, and among other sentences, he wrote these:

"During multiple rocket-launcher fires, the two shell-shocked trembling creatures forgot to hate each other. Who knows how many nights they spent together, embracing. Who knows how they survived. I imagine the cat hunted and fed the dog pigeons, mice, little rabbits. And when the cat couldn't catch anything, perhaps Fritz did. Or maybe they ate horse carcasses, or even human corpses. I don't want to imagine that. I am sure they didn't—they hunted. I see Bobo hunt in the yard in the morning. But the strange thing is, they don't let me approach them. They don't let me into the house, either. Anyhow, all I want to say is: if Fritz and Bobo get along, why couldn't we?"

That was a rhetorical question. Igor didn't expect an answer, but three weeks later—not much longer than it took the letter to reach Belgrade—Dara arrived on a seemingly empty train. People didn't dare to travel at night in the trains, and if they did, they lay on their seats and on the floors for fear of snipers.

Once she closed the squeaking yard-gate of her old home, Dara hugged her husband. Fritz and Bobo came out of the house and growled at them.

A VARIATION ON A THEME OF BOCCACCIO

DURING THE TIMES of Jacob the Patriarch, love was made passionately and blindly so that Jacob and, undoubtedly, many other men could not make out a difference between two radically different-looking women in their beds. During the Renaissance, wives couldn't tell the difference between husbands and other men, a failing which gave rise to sensual jubilations.

Nowadays, in our passionless age of electricity and information, people notice every little difference, detail by detail, eliminating all the hope of passing for someone else in bed.

I cursed the age I lived in when I met a bewitching woman, wife of an Episcopal minister, at an anti-nuclear rally in the city of C. When a crew of cripples from the suburbs of Nagasaki rolled in electric wheelchairs across the podium, she searched through her snakeskin purse for a handkerchief or paper tissue. I handed her my handkerchief, a hand-woven memento from Athens, which I carried around for cultural value, and only in extreme emergencies did I blow my nose in it. She wiped her large tears, sun in her eyes and on her golden necklace, and the refracting and glittering radiance of her tears and blue eyes knocked a modern darkness out of my soul.

"Thou hast ravished my heart with one of thine eyes, with one chain of thy neck," I said to her, and her teeth shone. I wrote letters to her—her name was M (more I should not reveal)—in a combination of Gothic and Japanese calligraphy, in King James English, jealously hating the minister. I became poetic, lyrical, subtle, crass; my whole character bloomed with many contradictories of passion and imagination. But for one hundred pages of my imageries, which wept in ink from swan feathers in my fingers over waxed paper resembling papyri, she replied cursorily in a laser-printed PC Line font. "I appreciate your letters though they shock me. I've never received such lyrical gibberish in my whole life. Please, don't ever write to me like that again. You may write to me if you wish, if you have something to say, especially on the non-radioactive fusion research you do."

I no longer sprinkled verses from ancient texts onto my page, such as, "Thy teeth are as a flock of sheep that are even shorn, which come up from washing, whereof every one bear twins." I wrote about the absolute power of the forces of attraction among nuclear particles, thinking she needed a cover lest her husband should perchance read something incriminating. After I explained to her the turmoil my bottle-fusion experiment was undergoing at the hands of envious colleagues with billion-dollar reactors, she yielded to my invitation to take a boat ride on a lake, but did not respond to my attempt to kiss her—or rather, she did, recoiling from me so abruptly that the boat tilted and she fell overboard. I pulled her out by her narrow wrist. Through her silk, I saw the outline of Aphrodite, her nipples scolded with the cold, erect. The minute blond hairs on her breasts stood up, alarmed. But from the Neoclassical body a modern and gruff voice shouted, "I don't wish to see you ever again! You are so single-minded!"

And true enough, I was single-minded, able to think of nothing but her form. My yearning took various shapes, but alas, none that would please her, because they all were the variations of me and not of my brother.

I've delayed to mention—I was so loath to interrupt the illusion of another beginning that writing about the beginning gave me—that M slept with her husband rarely, and with my brother often. My brother, an endowed chair in chemistry at our pompous university, had been with me at that no-nuke rally, and instead of writing letters on papyri, he had called her up on a cordless phone from his Turbo Saab.

Delicate M's sleep was fragile, and so at home she slept in a bedroom of her own on the second floor, in the western suburbs of the city of C, among pines, oaks, crew-cut golf courses of subtle green shades, dark ponds with pink water lilies. Tiger-striped black and orange bees rubbed their legs in gentle dust in red flowers, completing the colors of the German flag. In a nearby botanical garden, trees swooned promiscuously in balmy winds, casting their aromatic pollens. Near her window bowed an all-knowing oak. Its branches richly bifurcated and trifurcated so that my brother easily climbed into her room, to come home with floridly lurid details. "Oh, Joachim, her lips are so smooth and moist, you can see lust rippling in microwaves over them before I bite her ear and pass my incisor through her pierced earlobe. And her nether lips…"

For jealousy I heard buzzing in my ears, and in darkness saw frozen winter moss on the northern side of a beech in the forest of my distant childhood. And the Bible echoed, "Jealousy is cruel as the grave; the coals thereof are coals of fire which hath a most vehement flame."

If only I looked like my brother! We did look alike, but never had anybody mistaken me for him. I thought him uglier, though his head was full of hair and mine wasn't. I photographed him and took the photos to a wig designer. No sooner had I got the dreadfully expensive wig than my brother cut his hair.

I wasn't about to give up. Our hairs were approximately of the same length and color, but mine was curly, his flat. My hairline had retreated far from the slopes of my forehead; his hadn't budged.

I got a hair transplant. I gained what I wished to gain anyhow. If Steve had been balding and I'd had a full head of hair, I would have had to pluck my hair, just for the slim hope of tricking M. Yet I would have done it.

In a black ghetto parlor, a barber ironed and straightened my hair. Now I could hope to deceive M, the way Jacob had deceived Isaac, passing for his brother Esau.

But that was only a beginning. My nose was straight, thin, long, classically so. Art curators used to compliment me on it. My brother's broken nose looked like the Black Monday graph, horizontal with a sudden long drop. I went to a scar-faced plastic surgeon who had lifted many a famous cheek. I showed him Steve's nose. "Sir Doctor, I'd like to have one just like that."

"Are you demented?" He touched my nose, gazed obliviously, and said, "You must be putting me on, you know my weakness!"

"I wish I were." I was dejected, for I was fond of my nose.

"Young man, you've no idea how much I love money, yet still, I beg you not to do it. Walk as an example of what a nose should look like."

"Please, hurry up with the job!"

"How about changing something else? I could make your eyes slanted, heighten your cheekbones..." He clearly assumed that I wanted to change my appearance because I must have done some terrible crime, which was not true, not at that time anyhow.

He cut out a piece of my nose, smashed and twisted the rest, and despite all the painkillers, it was a crucifixion. But with each bang on the nose, I was closer to my beloved's breath, which would balm me like a dewy wind from the cedars of Lebanon.

After my physical recovery—I did find out how much the doctor loved money, I couldn't hope to recover financially yet—in the mirror my brother gazed at me from around the swollen nose. I kept the nose pinched in bandages and wore a baseball cap. Steve thought I had been through a bad neighborhood.

Steven was a bit heftier than I. So I gorged on meat like a Tatar, slept like a lion, melted Turkish delights on my tongue like a sultan. In three weeks, Steve and I looked like twins.

My changed looks could get me as far as her bed. But in our merciless age, you have to talk before caressing, and only when it seems you have nothing more to say, you make love. My voice would hinder me.

I modulated my voice, but, to get his lisp, I needed to eliminate a premolar. My dentist made me sign that I wouldn't sue him, and he doubled the regular extraction fee, for the legal risk. It's one thing to have a sick tooth pulled, there is even pleasure in the painful departure of pain—but to have sturdy roots torn from the nerves and the blood vessels! The dentist grinned with gusto as my tooth and my jaw crackled, and he chatted with his mini-skirted assistant about the computer-balanced Pirellis on his Jaguar. When my gum ceased to bleed, while the insides of my jaw still itched, I copied Steve's lisp perfectly.

In the meanwhile, I had neglected my nuclear fusion. Most traditional nuclear physicists, in fear of losing multimillion-dollar support from the military, railed against the Salt Lake City physicists, who overshadowed me, but some railed against me most acrimoniously, claiming that I was faking my data. I had recorded even more energy release than the Lake researchers. Ever since M had ravished me with her eyes, I didn't care to defend myself, though I believed I had found the key that would redeem not only me and the Lake physicists but all of modern humanity—we'd have more cheap and safe energy than we could put to use. But then, is there such a thing as safe energy?

My love wasn't safe energy. For love is strong as death.

The hair, nose, and the lisp would carry me into her embrace. And then? I remembered that unlike me, Steve was circumcised. Where was I to get a circumcision? I had already spent too much money. If only I were a Jew! Well, why not become one?

I went to a synagogue. My conscience pricked me for abusing the sacred for the secular, but then, is love secular?

The rabbi questioned me, and I gave my apology. "I don't believe in Christ. Yet I still have a burning religious want, a faith in one G-d, whose guidance I long for."

He lamented that most modern Jews, converts included, took religion as a cultural mainstay rather than a communion with G-d. "Incidentally, if you aren't, are you willing to be circumcised?"

"Oh, yes, longing to be!" He flipped his sharp eyebrow skeptically and curled his soft side lock contemplatively. "Is it expensive?" I asked.

"It's free, but at your age, it can be tremendously painful. Why don't you think about it, lest you enter the covenant rashly."

To convince him and myself—each step on my thorny path to her ruffled lips absorbed me completely—I studied Hebrew while gorging on cheap steroid beef. Three weeks afterward, I reappeared at the synagogue, reciting to the rabbi the first chapter of Genesis in strong consonants. The contemplative rabbi's eyes lit up with Mediterranean alertness. He recommended me to the regional board, whose rabbinical members asked more about my learning Hebrew than about my plagiarized theology.

What torture! The skin capable of creating pleasure turned out more capable of inflicting pain. It stayed sore for two weeks, and I still shivered at the thought of unsheathing.

I could now groan at M's nostrils and lick the hairs in her nose. But, though I could speak like Steve—I copied his syntax and vocabulary—I didn't know whether I could groan Steve-like.

On the Fourth of July, certain that the patriotic zeal had carried everybody out to stare at the pinks, reds, and crackling yellows in the burnt sky, I hid a microphone among the rugged leaves of the old oak. I stretched the dark brown wires through the bark grooves to the cubic hedges at the lily pond, where I hid among creaking toads. Love shuns no debasements, yet I loathed my eavesdropping as my brother gripped M's sternocleidomastoid muscle in his teeth.

The evening before his next scheduled visit, about which he routinely bragged, I said to him, "Brother, let's celebrate!"

"Celebrate what?"

"I've converted to Judaism."

"Are you nuts? What for? Jews will always consider you second rate, respecting you less than before, and Gentiles will think you third rate. Shifting identities, you'll lose your character, nobody will respect you!"

"But I am sincere. I enjoy the Old Testament. Physics gains strength from mystical Judaism, and I've always wanted to be a Wandering Jew."

Steve jeered. He smoked a brown Cuban cigar, sticking out the very tip of his tongue through his lips when the strong leaves smarted its lick-sores. I brought out several bottles of Rothschild wine from the end of the Great War, whereupon my brother changed his mind about my conversion.

I sipped. He gulped, quickly replenishing his glass. He rubbed the glass edge, making the high sound ring from the vibration. When his droopy-eyed head dropped onto his forearm, I dragged him to his bed and roped him.

In the morning, he shrieked. I told him that upon drinking wine with him, M had tied him. Inscrutable are the ways of love.

"Damn your jokes. Tonight I have to visit her! Untie me!"

"The undulating lips will always ripple for you." I took off my nose cover and my baseball cap. His face darkened into the color of the wine he'd so amply drunk.

My heart beat in luscious fright while I climbed the tree and dug my nails into the bark like a cat. In the window, veiled behind a silky curtain, she whispered, and I heard, "Come , I have decked my bed with coverings of tapestry, with carved works, with fine linens from Egypt. I have perfumed my bed with myrrh, aloes, and cinnamon. Come, let us take our fill of love until the morning." I hastened as a bird to its snare, as a hawk to its dove.

Upon leaping over the ledge, I flung myself into her embrace, kissed her ear with tenderest violence that flowed through my lip toward her lips; my jaws quivered with their power.

"You taste different tonight, but...mmm! What have you eaten?"

"Turkish delight. I love you now more than ever!" I lisped in the voice of my brother. Yet I couldn't stop my tongue from shaping, in Hebrew, "Thy two breasts are like two young roes that are twins, which feed among the lilies. Until the day break, and the shadows flee away..." I quit, afrighted—this was out of Steve's line—yet she heard nothing but my throaty lust. I savored her flesh, cool petals from the lily pond, through the silk that enshrouded her in a pink cloud in the pale moon's silent rays. I freed myself from my rude linen and entwined my flesh with the ghost of my fantasy, her flesh. I strove into the confluence of all my yearning, into the emptiness inside the crystalline form of blood—she was a blood crystal.

"Wow, I want you like the first night, Steve!"

It reassured and yet disturbed me that she sighed my brother's name.

We were drowning in the tormenting thrill, in the waves of seething lust. I sought fullness by emptying my bones in the focus of her misty beauty, to capture her elusive haze into a definite form of my will transcending itself. She sought to catalyze her dream, her haze, by my clear will, luring my will to leap out of itself, so she would seal it in her fullness of being. A flash of ecstasy—the sheets of lightning trembling out there on the horizon and inside, in my teeth, my nose, my hair, my gone foreskin. I felt like a scorpion, dying upon emitting the sting. What post-orgasmic repose! M's fingernails slid over my navel. Now that I had gone through the death cycle, the touch perturbed me. I wished no resurrection yet. I wished nothing to be added or taken away, and nothing to stir.

She whispered, "Steve, Steve, oh, Steve!" At that, my lacerated ego awoke, like an owl with the sinking of the sun. "Oh, Steve." Out of her tongue the serpent from the garden of Eden hissed through my ear, scratching the skin on my Adam's apple. My hairs stood up in proud, cold rebellion on my prickly skin.

"I am Joachim. I have only playacted Steve. But I am..."

"Stop, Steve!"

"Joachim. I have changed my nose, hair, teeth."

"You aren't..."

"I learned how to imitate. So much for the inimitable love! Steve. No. Spurned Joachim. Haha." She paled away. I reveled.

"Mean bastard!" she said.

"Your misplaced love has twisted me into a bastard brother. Yet you have just loved me."

"No, I love Steven."

"You loved all the little changes in style, in passion—all quintessentially mine. I don't care what you say. I tasted your truth!"

She sobbed. I took no pity on her. With the nonchalance of the one who has transcended a case of love, I crawled down the tree, naked, my nails in the bark, my skin tearing against thorny protrusions. With moonlight upon my skin, tranquil, I walked with my blessing to my foolish brother Esau.

I untied him. He flew in the chains of love to the tired oak, like a hungry monkey to a coconut tree. Although I was not curious—I merely strutted in the pine-needled breeze—I heard their voices: sharp, rising, ever sharper, in a quarrel. Soon another voice joined, M's husband. Furniture crashed. He must have woken at my unabashed ecstasy, and he waited, used to humiliation, until he could take it no more. When Steven returned, his left knuckles bled; he had struck out the minister's two front teeth in exchange for the minister's smashing his crooked nose—now it was straight! —and plucking out his hair.

With the sounds of Carmina Burana on my stereo, I looked at Steven, who looked like I used to. He'd even lost his taste for fine wines. I laughed, and my cheer grew better and better with the tart oaky taste of the old red wine on my tongue, although the oak did taste rotten.

AN OLD DEBT

BORIS WALKED UP to Stephan, a Gypsy in his late thirties, at an outdoor café in the park of Nizograd, Yugoslavia, and said, "You remember, you owe me money."

"This is not the time to talk about it. Why should you remind me of it now? And in public. That's an insult."

"I didn't mean it as an insult. But it's twelve years since I gave you two hundred German marks—I was a kid then and gave you all my savings so you could get your wife from Bulgaria to Yugoslavia, and it's high time you returned it."

"Why are you speaking of such private matters here in public? That definitely is an insult. Let's go out and fight," Stephan said. The park was enshrouded in a musty mist after the rain.

There was a liter mug of foamy beer in front of Stephan, and two others with foam at the bottom. His eyes were bloodshot. A pink knife scar ran diagonally over his brown forehead. He was standing up slowly, stroking the side of his black jacket as if to ascertain his knife was where it should be.

Boris had no knife and he didn't want to find out whether Stephan had one. Boris was in better physical shape; he worked in West Germany as a Gastarbeiter in the Bayerische Motoren Werke near Munich. A fight would attract the police, who, knowing Boris worked in the West, would detain him out of malice longer than his vacation and he'd lose his job. If he won the fight, he'd still lose.

Stephan was already standing, and shouting, "Why are you waiting? Let's go into the woods where nobody can see us." Dozens of people were smoking silently, watching them. Boris was glad that the people listened to them, because that was some sort of protection, and yet he was not glad, because the situation was embarrassing.

"I have no reason to fight," said Boris.

"I have a reason to: you insulted me."

"I didn't intend to insult you; without intention, there is no insult."

"There is. The fact that you showed so little respect, that you think I am a Gypsy bum, that came across, and that is an insult. Now we have no way out."

"You being a Gypsy makes no difference. Gypsies are people just like everybody else."

"See, I told you, you are a chauvinist. We'll have to fight it out."

"You talk nonsense."

"Come on, let's fight; do me the favor; I want to kill you."

"Calm down. I didn't intend to insult you, and I don't care about the money that much. It wouldn't make sense to fight for so little money—life is not so cheap."

"You'd be surprised how cheap life can get. And you are insulting me again by publicly mentioning that I owe you money. I don't owe you nothing. I don't owe nobody in the world nothing. The whole world can fuck itself, and you to begin with. But it's nice of you that you say we don't owe nothing to each other. Very nice. We could be friends again."

"I have no desire to be friends with you."

"Oh, come on, couldn't we be friends?" He bulged his large eyeballs, the color of tobacco, jaundiced, with burst capillaries. "Waiter, bring us two mugs!"

Two mugs of beer promptly whirled down on the table, some foam spilling and soaking into the white cloth, hissing or whispering, "Shhh," as if asking for silence.

Stephan clanked his mug against Boris's, which stayed untouched on the table. The tension was suspended, on hold, and Boris looked into the bubbles swerving to the surface and joining the foam. The lower layer of foam was all made of little bubble balls, resembling a spawning ground of small fish. He wondered how it was possible to be in his shoes now, a little bubble who strove to rise high as a kid by being a good Christian, by giving all his money to the poor man he vaguely knew, and instead of rising to the top, he was stranded somewhere meaningless, petty, not even receiving gratitude for that one redeeming moment of goodness. He received outrage instead! He remembered how Stephan had played a cracked guitar on a park bench not far from where they were sitting now, playing Mexican songs with tears in his eyes, in his throat. Boris, touched, had run home, bringing back all his red and blue banknotes.

Boris daydreamed now, recalling Stephan's little brother, who had been a few grades below Boris, but couldn't remember his name. The pupils had always left their shoes lined up against the wall in the corridor—they used cloth slippers in the classroom—and shoes now and then disappeared. Since the brother used to leave class before the end of the lessons, he had often been accused of stealing the shoes. Once, he stood in front of the whole class, barefoot, weeping, his hair disheveled, his shirt not tucked in, the smallest boy in the class, and the teacher slapped his cheeks and whipped his opened palms with a willow branch, shouting, "Admit it, dirty Gypsy, you've stolen the shoes!" The boy swore he didn't and got whipped more. The teacher searched his bag. The shoes were not there. She made the whole class search everywhere in the yard for the hidden shoes that Stephan's brother had stolen.

After the beating, the brother missed school for two weeks, and when he came back on a snowy day, he was barefoot. He couldn't have stolen the shoes: he would have worn them. Wasn't he beaten because he was a Gypsy? Boris recalled how he too beat the boy once to find out whether it was true what he had been told, that Gypsies were nimble fighters. He had dragged the boy, half his size, all around the greasy floor of the classroom, and choked him under the teacher's desk. When the teacher came, she made only the brother—and not Boris—kneel in the corner over corn kernels. The brother dropped out of school after that year, the fifth grade.

"Cheers!" Stephan knocked his glass against Boris's, now in Boris's hands, and they drank, not looking each other in the eye. "So, ready to fight now?"

"You change like the weather."

"You know, you left for Germany and you never even sent me a card. Never mind; I forgive you. Really, in this town I have no friends. Let's be friends again."

"It would take a lot of restoration of trust..."

"Come on, I was only joking about fighting. Trust is a good thing. Banks are called trusts in many countries, the world cannot live without trust. I hope you trust me, do you trust me?" Stephan again stroked the sides of his jacket.

"Sure, I can trust you."

"Can. Do you? Many things can be, but what's the fact?"

"All right, I trust you," Boris said, disgusted with the mind games and with his lack of courage, his paranoia about the police, wondering whether he shouldn't simply fight, be a man. He was shocked he was now being threatened, and it seemed to him that he perversely liked it, though equally perversely he would have liked to cut Stephan's throat so that his greenish face would become purple.

"If you trust me," said Stephan, "prove it. I hear you want to buy some Hungarian currency…"

"How do you know that?" Boris asked in astonishment. It was true: Boris was getting ready to spend the rest of his vacation in Hungary.

"How do I know that? Ha! I know more about you than you think, some things that not even you know!" To punctuate his statement, he raised his eyebrows and contemptuously snorted. "So, my dear friend, why don't you exchange two hundred German marks for my forints. I have them; we Gypsies have special connections with Hungary."

"Well, what's your exchange rate?"

"One mark is twenty forints in the bank. I'll give you a beautiful exchange rate—forty forints. You cannot find any better than that." His throaty voice was persuasive.

Boris found it comfortable to think about the exchange rates rather than about their bizarre conflict, and as he thought about the money, suddenly he began to think it would be good to get a lot of forints. He could live like a lord in Hungary for a week. "Yes, the rate is good, but I don't have the money here."

"Where do you have it? At home? I'll walk you home."

"All right," Boris said, though he was not sure he wanted the exchange. "You have the money here?"

"Greedy, aren't you? Yes, I have it."

Boris was about to ask him to show it, but Stephan winked at him, smiled, and said: "Trust, remember? If you test, you don't trust."

As they walked to Boris's, Stephan said, "You know, it's probably just as well we didn't fight. We can be good friends."

Boris said nothing to that.

"But if we fought—of course we'd damage each other, knock out a tooth or two, break noses, see my nose? Pretty crooked, isn't it? I broke noses more times than mine was broken."

"I don't want to break your nose or teeth, nor mine. It's expensive to get a new tooth," Boris said.

"How expensive is it in Germany?"

"One thousand marks."

"Wow, you do live in the promised land, don't you? That much just for a rotten tooth! You should be thankful I haven't knocked out your teeth. Still, it's a pity we didn't fight. Maybe someday we'll correct that. You know, after a fight, we could get drunk and really make friends. If you've nearly killed each other, then you know where you stand, and next time you just laugh about your troubles. You are closer than brothers. These friendships last for life, you know." He spoke in a lamenting voice, tears in his eyes, as if they had missed something wonderful.

"I am not sure about that," Boris said.

"And how come we are walking? Don't the Germans give you a BMW to drive around?"

"Well, yes, but I flew in, it's less bother."

"Oh, you flew in, it's less bother," Stephan mimicked with mock sympathy.

Boris was thinking of saying that he didn't want to exchange any money. But Stephan looked crazy, beery foam was in the corners of his mouth and tears rolling down his cheeks. "My friend, you'd have no way of running away; my brothers would find you or I would find you anywhere in the world. We like to travel."

Boris looked at him askance. What the hell was the root of that emotion in Stephan's voice and eyes? It had nothing to do with his words.

Boris felt like a fool as he handed out two hundred marks into one of Stephan's hands. Stephan's other hand stayed in the pocket. At first Boris thought nothing of it, expecting Stephan would hand him the Hungarian money nearly simultaneously. But, as the money parted from his fingers, Boris felt a bit of a void in his stomach. Stephan began to laugh and said, "So there we go again. In all these years, you've learned nothing!"

"Where are the forints?"

"What forints? Well, in Hungary there are a lot! Oh, yes, I'd quite forgotten. Tonight I'll be at the Park Café to give you the money. Everything. But if I am not there, then I fooled you, you hear? I owe you nothing. I outsmarted you; that's fair. It's time you learned some basics. Private education is expensive."

"True, I was dumb about this whole thing, but you didn't outsmart me. You said things were based on trust."

"That's where you were outsmarted. You did not trust me. If you had, it would have been a balanced exchange. See, I trusted you all the way, that's why I came ahead. Well, my friend, I had a great time with you, it's time to shake hands."

Stephan pursed his lips and closed his eyes as if to kiss Boris. Boris shrank back.

In the evening Boris was having a wiener schnitzel at the Park Café, drinking red wine, curious as to whether Stephan would show up to return some of the money or to try to get more. Boris felt humiliated the whole evening as he drank with his friend Davor, who talked about the need to introduce the free market economy and multi-party system as a means of checks and balances. Boris didn't listen, and he couldn't confide what had gone on because he feared he would sound like a chauvinist, filled with prejudice, postjudice—generalization from too few facts, which was worse than prejudice. He thought he could say, "I know there are bad people among all the races, why should the Gypsies be any different?" Not even that would do.

I should not call anybody a Gypsy. The new name is Roma. But I am not used to the new name. What difference does a name make? Nothing makes a difference here. It's an all-around dehumanizing experience. Or a humanizing one. All real experience is a humanizing one.

A cool breeze flowed out of the woods, and Boris could see the clear sky, even the haze of the Milky Way was somehow clear. Boris chewed the steak and said, "This is like licking and chewing boots."

"That's right, Boro," said Davor, trying to fit a lens, smeared with his arching fingerprints, back into his glasses frame. "You don't feel it, but here we live like dogs. We are the Third World right here in Central Europe. Why, we are Bolivia—we've moved to South America with our inflation. All we have is our rain forest!" Davor laughed. "And why? The Serbs have squeezed out of Croatia all the foreign currency we make by tourism and exports. As long as the Serbs rule Croatia...the national problem..."

Boris stared. What was this? Chauvinism? A just complaint? Why all this obsession with Serbs?

The next morning, hung over, Boris sat in front of the milk bar at the center of the town, blinking, observing the passers-by, carrying on the conversation with Davor and pondering the night before.

How could Stephan turn out to be such a crook? He is probably faithful and law-abiding within his community, but owes no obligation to the white, Slavic community that suspects him, scorns him, excludes him. I was somehow condescending, as I had been doing him the favor all the way along, talking to him. But there was some beauty in it all. I was being humiliated, but I said to myself, let him exploit me, let me be humiliated like a whimsical character from a Russian novel, that is, a novel by Dostoevsky and not Tolstoy—don't people always mean a novel by Dostoevsky when they say "a Russian novel"?

Boris felt there was something dishonest in his explanation of the incident; he wanted to give it a certain polish.

Davor in the meanwhile talked on. "And nobody can find jobs here anymore. Serbian managers sell machinery and entire factories to foreigners, who dismantle them. We find part-time jobs, or none, or we smuggle from abroad. The concept of honesty has changed..."

Just then from around the corner appeared Stephan with a barefoot, messy-haired boy of about ten, his son. The two walked into a shoe store, and reappeared a couple of minutes later, the boy hopping in a pair of Pumas and the father looking on with glistening eyes and smiling broadly.

Boris smiled too, unburdened.

YAHBO THE HAWK

INSTEAD OF TO THE CHURCH, I walked one Sunday morning to the nearby park. Just as I was about to climb an oak, I saw my friend Peter walking down the path beside a grim partisan monument.

Peter used to lead Catholic funeral processions, holding a varnished cross, dressed in white vestments, his checks pink in the wind or the heat, while a priest sang in monotonous Latin. I respected Peter for his knowledge of Latin, which still did not prevent me from cornering him in our classroom and punching him like a boxing sack. I rented him for that purpose, a dinar for ten minutes of practice. Peter now carried a covered pleated basket.

"What have you got there?" I asked him.

"If you want to find out, give me five dinars."

I gave him a bronze dinar coin and peeped in.

"Don't open much; they might fly away!"

"What are they? Little ravens?"

"No. Can't you see? Hawks."

"And what will you do with them?"

"I don't know. Feed my dog."

"Look, why don't you give them to me?"

"Give. Are you crazy? They're not easy to come by!"

"Well, what do you want for a hawk?"

"It's a precious bird. You could train it to catch chickens, one a day, which would make three hundred and sixty-five chickens a year, and with that you could buy all kinds of things…"

"I'll give you my sword."

"Come on! We outgrew that."

"My sweater and my jeans?"

"They would be too tight on me."

"You could stretch them."

"No, forget it!"

And he pretended he would walk on.

"How about a strawberry ice cream?"

Now I had him. His mouth began to water. He swallowed saliva, his eyelids drooped. "Three!"

We walked to the sweets shop. I bought him three ice creams and he lapped them like a cat drinking milk. Then he took out one hawk. I gripped it to make sure its talons, small Turkish sabers turned upside down, could not reach me. I was uneasy about the beak.

"I'd like the other hawk too!"

"That would be ten almond ice creams."

"How about three egg-cream cakes?"

"Four!" he said.

I searched through my pockets, and in the mess of nails, wires, cigarette butts, and several round pebbles for throwing at traffic signs and teacher's windows, I found one torn red piece of paper with a picture of a muscular factory worker on it.

"Let that be a deposit!"

I rushed home with the hawk in my hands, held far in front of me.

The hot bird pulsated with fast heartbeats; its whole body was one big heart with sharp edges and eyes atop its valves. As soon as I got home, I put it into a cupboard, stole some money that was kept in a prayer book to ensure divine protection, and ran back to the sweets shop.

Peter was not there. I learned later that he sold the bird to a cop's son, Nik. Next time I ran into Peter, I said, "Look, I paid for the hawk, and you gave it away. Get the hawk back from Nik!"

"No, I want to be on good terms with him and his father because I still need to steal some things…"

"All right, this is for the deposit!" I gave him a black eye, to which he responded by giving me a wonderful show of the firmament, with more stars than there are sons of Abraham, Isaac, and Jacob—a black eye of my own. In all fairness to the art of painting, which takes time, I must say that his eye was not yet black but red and purple, the following day it was green and yellow, and on the third day it was blue. Now I knew that you could get green out of blue and yellow, but that you could get blue out of green and yellow was a novelty, and it was not an exception proving the rule, because the area surrounding my eyes followed the same revolutions of color as his. In the end our colors were dark blue, like the most common sort of plums. Ashamed of my plum-eye, for four days I joined the pirates, wearing a greasy strap of leather across my head.

At home in the attic, my hawk's new home, I waited till my eyes would get used to the darkness. I made out the bird's silhouette on a crossbeam; it was emerging from the dark, like a picture developed in a lab, sharper and sharper. It turned sideways toward me. When I began to approach the silhouette, it jumped and flapped its wings unsteadily to another beam. It nearly fell from the beam onto the bales of cowhide that my father had used for making clogs before his death. Along the walls of the attic, there were piles of wooden soles; newspapers and magazines, some with pictures of Russian spaceships and dogs, and one of Marilyn Monroe with her lips parted; jigsaw puzzles with missing pieces; and a flat leather soccer ball.

I christened the hawk Yahbo, a man's name, feeling like Adam in paradise naming the animals. I was not sure what Yahbo's gender was, though I wanted to think of him as male. Still, I didn't ruffle through its feathers to find out, fearing that afterward I'd have to rely only on my sense of touch, the beak and talons making my eyes flutter at the thought of coming close to them.

In the back of the attic, sunshine streaked in, stronger and stronger, and particles of dust were brilliant, burning like stars in a downward Milky Way. Through the window, facing east, you could see the mountains and forests from which Yahbo must have come, from a no doubt very noble lineage stretching all the way from the Garden of Eden and God's breath. If He made Adam of soil, He made hawks of leaves, detached leaves that winds carried aloft; with God's breath reaching them, the leaves ceased to be the helpless toys of the winds, and instead the stems evolved into seeing heads, and the outer edges into wings. And so came into being the great surveyor of forests, from the leaves' soft riblets.

I brought him water to drink. But he would not drink. I fed him liver meat, a quarter of a pound. I paid attention that it be bathed in blood because otherwise he would not get enough liquids. It was hot in the attic.

Several days later, Yahbo sat on a crossbeam and stared. White film was covering his eyes, slowly, and withdrawing back somewhere beneath the hairs around his eyes. His beak was half open. He is dying of thirst and grief, I thought. I went to the library to find out whether young hawks drank water, or blood only, and I wasn't able to find anything on the topic. Since he would not drink water from a pot, I went to the junkyard behind the local hospital, where there were all kinds of syringes. I filled one with water and aimed a squirt into Yahbo's beak. Water would not pass down his throat. Drops trickled from his beak onto the dusty floor and coated themselves in dust, squirming and curling on the ground like miniature hedgehogs. I dropped all shyness with Yahbo, grabbed his neck and squirted into his beak, again and again, until his Adam's apple went up and down without water spilling out of his beak. Afterward, he learned to drink from a pot of water. On hot days he soaked his legs and dipped his wings. He shook all his feathers, water flying around the attic. He dipped his head in the pot too.

Yahbo was growing rapidly. I wanted to teach him to sit on my shoulder and to love me so he would not fly away into his forests, never to return. I wanted to walk with him on my forearm wrapped in ox hide. He would attack those who displeased him and pluck out their eyes with his talons, tear their ears off or at least pierce through them, making holes for earrings.

It was already summer, and since there was no school, it was the busiest time of the year for soccer, biking, and reading. I often forgot to feed Yahbo for days. Suddenly remembering my neglect, I would run to the butcher's.

Even the hours I did have to train Yahbo I did not know how to put to use. I made a leather strap for my forearm. But Yahbo would not sit on it, growing irritated with my trying to place him there. A couple of times his beak started toward my eyes so I had to cast him aside. I am sure he had no sentimental impulses to kiss my ears or play with my hair locks—it was my eye he wanted to drink.

I imagined I should take him out when he was starved and tease him with some meat on a whirling rope, and he would fly after it in circles, and learn to stay around me. But the taste of freedom, I thought, would be sweeter to him than blood.

To Yahbo I was a jailer more than a friend. I could not talk to him. He would not look at me. His head was always tilted sideways so I didn't know where he was looking. Perhaps he was looking at me, but I couldn't tell, and that did not do much for communication between us. Nor did he trust me. When I walked into the attic, he would often fly from the front beam far back into the darkest recesses under the roof. But sometimes he flew from the recesses toward me and let me approach him if I moved slowly. I caressed him down his feathers, with a quickening sensation in my whole body. Petting Yahbo was like petting a sword with sharp double edges, a perfect smooth cold surface over which you glide your palms. But he was not cold, he was very warm and soft. He seemed quite pleased then, his eyes growing shiny, teary, radiant hazel. His head moved a bit to the left and a bit to the right; he probably did not know what to think; was I being affectionate toward him? As if to ask me what it all meant, he opened his beak, but no sounds came out. In the beak I saw his thin red and pointed tongue, almost a snake's tongue. Overcome with sadness that he could not speak the language of humans, he stayed that way, his beak open, and the white film slid over his eyes like Venetian blinds.

I often stayed in the attic for hours, just staring at the majestic bird. He was growing so large that I thought he might be an eagle. I doubted whether I could train him. It did not seem that he would want to be a servant. He was born to be a master, a count of the heavens, and who was I? Son of a clog-maker. How should I subdue this nobility? If he were a son of a banal human nobleman, I would gladly lynch him and humiliate him daily, make his nose bleed and tie him to a tree, a post of shame, the way I did with the mayor's son.

After I'd been there for a long while, Yahbo would fly the whole length of the attic, swing around and smash straight into the glass window. Five laths of wood made twelve square glass surfaces too small to be shattered like that. Yahbo would fall to the floor, stand up, fly back to the opposite end of the attic, and in a couple of minutes he'd be flying again, pointing his body straight to pass through the space between the laths. And he would crash again.

In the morning he perched on the narrow ledge against the windowpanes, his beak open and uttering no sound, bewildered, perhaps not understanding what kind of air it was that would show you the wonders of your homeland and wouldn't let you pass through, homeward. He faced east like a Muslim toward Mecca or a Jew facing Jerusalem; for him the glass was the Wailing Wall.

Time and again he flew against the window so mercilessly I was scared he would break his neck. His eyes glowed with wrath. I was tempted to open the window for him, but did not.

He needed fresh, winged food. When my cat caught a sparrow, I stole it from her. I threw the croaking, shivering bird toward Yahbo, and Yahbo missed it, unprepared for hunting out of the blue. Then he swooped down at the quarry, picked it up and wildly flew with it around the attic several times, whereupon he landed on his favorite crossbeam, nailing the sparrow with his talons to the wood. He stood, dignified, with his head in profile, as if ready to be minted into a silver dollar or a German mark, or some other aggressive country's currency. Blood dripped from the beam onto the floor. Then Yahbo tore into the bird, his smaller nephew with the same color and same stripes as his own, and devoured it all, feathers, bones, eyes, everything, gulping hastily, his throat and eyes bulging out, and when his Adam's apple leaped over the last swallow, he seemed to regret that the pleasure was so short-lived.

Yahbo spread his wings like big arms of welcome. He opened his beak; his eyes increased in size and shot a beam of light; his snake tongue popped out. Then his body shook as if he were an alcoholic in delirium tremens. He opened his beak and vomited a chunk of feathers and blood. He cast another pallet. I ran downstairs to my mother in the kitchen.

"I have an upset stomach. Could you make me some garlic soup?"

"Of course you do. You take all the good food to that ugly bird."

She chopped cloves of garlic and tossed it into the boiling water with egg whites and charcoal bread. I put the soup in a syringe and spurted it into Yahbo's beak. He suffered it, now and then closing his beak to swallow and then opening it again, apparently asking for more.

Knowing that Yahbo needed fresh kill, I borrowed a rifle from a Hungarian boy, Janosh, with whom I fought nearly every day. I would hit him on the mouth, so his lips would be cut against his rabbit teeth; he'd fling chunks of coal, crushing my toes; I'd chase him through half the town, and, catching him by his long hair, choke him while he plunged his nails into my back until his hands grew weak and he seemed to swoon. Fearing for his safety, I'd release him, and he'd spring up and run away shrieking unprintable text. We were actually very good friends, and he lent me his rifle gladly.

I tiptoed into the beech forest, where I saw a weasel not far from me. I held my breath, slowly leaning the rifle barrel against the cold, peeled bark of a birch. The weasel did not seem to notice me. I aimed for the neck. Thup! The weasel jumped several times like a wild horse being tamed. I thought it would fall to the ground. It jumped onto another tree, almost missing a branch. I reloaded the rifle and followed. I tripped over a stump. I never lost sight of the weasel—its redness struggling to get onto another tree. I shot, missed, reloaded, shot, missed, reloaded. The weasel seemed to be picking up strength. I leaned against a tree and pulled the trigger. The weasel shook. It stood in one place trembling but would not fall. I must have put five more bullets into it, and it continued trembling. Then a spasm passed through its body, and it shook no more. But it would not fall.

Unsteadily I climbed up to the weasel. Its yellow fur was covered with blood, its neck torn, its eyes almost outside the sockets. I grabbed its bloody body and tore it off the branch and threw it to the ground. I slid down the beech bark and vomited. The green darkness grew darker and more radiant, and all I could see in the radiance was the red blood, screaming, like the blood of Abel, straight to God. I threw myself on the ground. I prayed to God, saying that I would never again kill any animals, except for mosquitoes, and ants that I was bound to step on—that I would never intentionally step on an ant, nor place, the way a friend of mine did, one ant's head against the neck of another to see an ant in panic biting through a sister's neck. I would beat a boy in my street for having bathed a cat in gasoline and set it on fire; I would beat a boy who lived two streets away from me, who had killed the black cat of a ninety-nine-year-old widow by putting it into the washing machine.

I promised God I would do all that on the condition that He restore life to the weasel. I waited, opened my eyes, and there was the weasel, as dead as before. I prayed more. I hit the ground with my fists, many times, until I hit something cool and slimy and when I opened my eyes, I saw I had squashed a snail. The weasel was still dead. I stood up, rubbed my slimy and bloody palm against the bark of the tree and against my jeans, and realized I had not completed my prayer. I said, "Amen!" The wind rustled around, invisible and ubiquitous, and the leaves trembled as it passed. With my bare hands I dug into the soft black soil; the soil stuck beneath my nails. I buried the weasel.

So I returned home empty-handed. Yahbo opened his beak, turned his head in many directions quickly, in expectation.

I saw that if I was going to let Yahbo go, I should not hesitate. It was already mid-August, and the more time passed, the more difficult it would be for him to learn how to hunt.

The following morning, with my bow and arrows, I pierced the carton of an empty box that had held sunflower oil bottles and put Yahbo into it. I tied a narrow sheet of tin around Yahbo's right foot, having inscribed on it my name and address with a needle. We set out for the mountains, the way Abraham set out with Isaac, to slaughter him as a burnt offering to God. I did not have the donkeys, so I had to be the donkey myself. I hoped that Isaac would live, that an angel would stop my raised hand with a knife in it. We went through the park, past the vineyards in the hills, through a layer of beeches into an oak forest. On the way I saw no hawks and wondered how he would do, whether he would find any company.

In a windless meadow, I opened the box. He jumped out awkwardly, more like a chicken than a hawk. He flapped with his wings vigorously, making a wind like a helicopter during take-off. He flew in a semicircle and perched on the branch of a bumpy cedar.

Everything had changed now. He was free. I was merely a human with bare hands, and flap as much as I would, I could not fly. He hesitated, fearing perhaps that there was a glass barrier somewhere against which he would smash and then fall back onto the sandy floor of the stuffy attic. After several minutes of contemplating the forest and the sky, he sprang from the branch. He flapped up in circles, higher and higher, spiraling into the heavens. High above me he glided on a new wind, keeping his wings still for a long time. Then he made a circle out of which he darted straight for the mountain.

Every day I went to the attic and through the eastern window I stared toward the mountain, and wondered where he was in the emerald temple. During thunderstorms I feared a lightning bolt would strike him because of the metal I had put on his right leg. It is said that friends are one soul in two bodies. Well, that one soul was not in me; it was circling somewhere above the trees over the mountain.

Two weeks later a local forester came by and told me that his dog had found a most peculiar thing: a dead hawk with a dead weasel in its talons. The hawk's talons were sunk in the hips of the weasel; the hawk had missed the neck he must have aimed for. The weasel's teeth were still in the hawk's breast. The forester gave me the entwined bodies.

I made a hole beneath the cedar to which Yahbo had flown. The tree roots were wiry and tough to cut through with my stone-age tool, a sharp stone. Among the roots I placed the thin limp mess of fur and dark blood of the weasel, for there it belonged.

Then I collected dry branches of trees, made a bundle on the ground, and put the limp chunk of feathers, flesh, beak, talons, and dark blood over it. The white film covered his eyes. From my pocket I took out the Psalms on thin fine paper. I crumpled the pages, set them under the pyre, and struck a match. The branches caught fire at once, crackling. The feathers smelled like a tire being burned. The flames fought through a thick layer of smoke and the smoke rose slowly. Some smoke touched my eyes, stung them; tears came out as if I had been gazing at a big naked onion. I took out a cigarette and lit it on the pyre. The circles of my smoke merged into Yahbo's smoke, and our smoke merged into the sky.

ACKNOWLEDGMENTS

GRATITUDE TO THE EDITORS of the journals where the stories first appeared:

"Honey in the Carcase," *Threepenny Review*
"Tumbleweed," *American Fiction Anthology*, ed. Tim O'Brien
"Wool," *Threepenny Review*
"Lies & Counter-Lies," *Apallachee Quarterly*
"Peak Experiences," *The Antioch Review*
"My Hairs Stood Up," *Gulf Coast*
"Charity Deductions," *New American Review*
"Fritz: A Fable," *Boston Review*
"A Variation on a Theme of Boccaccio," *Columbia Review*
"An Old Debt," *The Laurel Review*
"Yahbo the Hawk," *The New England Review*
"Obsession," *Narrative Magazine*

Some stories also appeared, in different form, in *Tumbleweed*, published in Canada by Vehicule Press. For time, space, and sustenance to write and revise these stories, the author thanks the Canada Arts Council, Fulbright Commission, Yaddo, Black Mountain Institute, The Hermitage Artist Retreat, Norton Island Eastern Frontier Retreat, OMI/Ledig House, Michael Saltman for the fellowship at the Black Mountain Institue and Next Page Foundation in Sofia.